M000029323

Dedicated to my old hockey teammates

Alex and Carson

CONCUSSED

Beanie hat season is back. The Barn blares rock music through its stereo system as the Kielstad Knights finish warmups. Parents pack the seats and surround the glass with their coffee cups in gloved hands. High schoolers tightly fill the corner of the stands next to the game doors. The rowdy ones stand at the top where the wooden backboard walls up. Can't wait to hear all of the physical abuse they put into it. That's why they got themselves a para eyeing them from the bottom. Strictly, we need more eyes for today's game. The Knights are playing the Dorcha Dragons. Dorcha's student section is also placed on the other side of the stairs from our section. Sure enough, there'll be a fist fight at some point. Hockey in Minnesota intensifies between both the players and audience. Gotta love it.

Mom's on the Kielstad bench, shaking hands with the referees. It's kind of strange having her as the head coach for the school, but it's comforting. A lot of memories rebound inside this metal shed. But now, she's standing where my dad used to stand. And the players, they play where I used to play. They also wear what I used to wear. One of the newer sophomore kids this year took my number. I'm a little on edge with it; he better not print poor possession with my number. 21.

Thomas. He finally gets to play starting goaltender his senior year. Ever since Cole graduated, and my mom became coach, Thomas has had the greatest opportunities this year. Their inching closer and closer to the middle of the season. It's December, about two weeks out from Christmas Day, and they'll be rolling over to Doug Wood Arena to play in the yearly post-Christmas tourney; that's the mark that hockey season is halfway done. Usually, Kielstad always loses the first game of the tourney, but maybe this year will be different with Thomas in net.

Boys from both teams skate around the net on smooth ice. Jake and Charlie conversate with Thomas by his net. I can't believe both of them are seniors this year. They're doing great at defense. Their chemistry makes for a perfect reaction. Play-by-play, it's tough to break their defensive wall. Defensive players need bodies of boulders on the ice, and that's exactly what they are. Not even dynamite can rupture the two. They've been friends for so long.

Friends. I've lost them over the past two years. Memories of Finn weathers in the wind as every day passes by. Chester still sulks in my thoughts. Orson soaks in my eyes every now and then. Shawn's death the most recent out of them all. But now Ash, he's left for his Army training. I won't be able to talk with him for months. The military rips the outside world from them, trapping them inside like a fish in a tank. Although, they're more likely trapped in a marsh or in the woods residing in South Carolina. Ash is over a thousand miles away.

Two kids chase each other down on the bleacher's walkway. From behind them, holding a tub of popcorn in his hands, shadows my new brother, Barrett. After what we witnessed at the hotel in town, I had no option but to ask him to stay with us. We're eighteen, so he's technically an adult now living on his own. I promised him that there's always a bed at our place. Sure, he may sleep in our creepy half-basement bedroom, but it's cozy having another warm soul under our roof. He keeps me sane when I need it most.

The melted butter on the freshly popped kernels whiffs into my nose as Barrett sits next to me.

"Is he here yet?" Barrett asks.

"I haven't seen him," says I.

The Dorcha Dragons and Kielstad Knights line up on their blue lines. They unstrap their helmets and face the flag in the front of The Barn. Everyone on the stands respects the flag for the National Anthem. The rock music softens as the voices hush around us. Students on the other hand always interrupt with their flat vocals, singing along with the pep band's music.

Pep band is organized in the corner by the game doors. The snare drums roll while the bass drum booms; the brass section hinters in the background with their low hums; the woodwinds harmonize one another, battling the deep brass' volume. And the student section converting into a choir adds sprinkles to the song.

Once the anthem finishes, the rock music rattles back on. Kielstad and Dorcha lap around their zones before bringing it in around the nets, prepping for their chant. It's gonna be exciting to see these new guys play against our rivals. Dorcha's coach looks like his old self with a scruffy beard from an ancient husky. If he catches me in the arena, I wonder if he'll recognize me. When we were at that cruddy orange arena, he made eye contact with me as he exchanged their team's accomplishments with Coach Kipp, gave me a smirk even. It's funny that high school hockey is done for me, but at the same time, the crumbs that resonate from the past come back one-by-one.

After the teams chant, the first liners get into position around the faceoff dot. One of the referees skates to the middle, signals the goalie and the score clock runner, then blows the whistle. The puck drops to the ice for the start of a riveting game. Kielstad wins the faceoff as they throw the puck back to Jake. Jake slides it to Charlie as they carry it over the neutral red line. Charlie sends the puck into the offensive zone as their forwards pressure the Dragons down low.

In the midst of all the cheering, footsteps shake the wood from under my feet. A boy in Dragon's clothing colored in black and orange strolls down the walkway. The orange, sowed-on 21 pops from his sweatpants.

"Thrasher!" says I. I stand from my seat for a gracious hug with him. Barrett does the same. While they hug, some of the parents shimmy their heads around our bodies. "Oops. Sorry." We kindly nestle our bodies back in our seats. It's quite tight on the bleachers, especially with a few more Dorcha students filling their fan section.

"So," Barrett says. "How have you been, Thrasher?"

"I've been doing fine," he says. "Been studying a lot recently for my upcoming exams. The college work picks up around Christmas break."

"You're going for a business degree, right?" says I.

"Yes," Thrasher says. "Business bachelor's degree, and then I'll move on to my masters. How bout you guys? Are you in college right now?"

Barrett responds, "I'm going to a private pilot school."

"I'm majoring in physical fitness online," says I. "Still planning on coaching in my future, but I thought this degree would work best in my nature too for a job."

"That's awesome," Thrasher says. "Guess summer helped you guys pick your paths." That's not something I'm fond on bringing up. Camp Kelmo was a shipwreck in our lives. I overheard rumors that the investigators are still suspicious with the cold case. The thought keeps my leg bouncing every month. How can anyone explain what happened there? A lot of useless deaths created by the one who disappeared from this world, burned to muck in the ground, stewed within the lava beneath the crust.

A Kielstad player slams a guy into the glass, right in front of the student section. Whistles blow in the frigid air, but the old tubular heaters hanging above us finally start to kick in with warmth. One of the younger players on our side is taken to the box for checking from behind. A rumbling in the walls disturbs me, timbering my anxiety to the floor. Glancing behind me, the rumbling and shaking of the bleachers comes from the students in the back, kicking and slamming the wooden backwall with their feet and hands. The loud sounds in here scar me with nightmares.

"Don't wanna do that again," says Thrasher. Every penalty in a hockey game triggers a little humor, especially after summer camp. It helps to laugh at the past, keeps me away from drowning in the waters with Orson. His parents locked themselves up for almost a month when they received the news, but they're slowly in the healing stage. Barrett and I met them last summer, we waited for the right time to show up to their front door. We mentioned to them that we were there for him, that me, Barrett, and Thrasher were with him the day he drowned. He wasn't alone.

A flash of light draws my eyes to the ceiling of The Barn. A new crystal disco ball spins above the faceoff dot. Danny probably forgot to turn it off after the figure skating practice. With all the hanging lights in The Barn, the disco ball is rarely a distraction, but it's surely going to distract me.

The hockey game resumes while Kielstad kills off their penalty. A penalty kill. Dorcha has the power in their hands with a one-man advantage. They benefit with a power play. It's a good thing Jake and Charlie play on the penalty kill as well as the power play. They'll get the puck iced all the way down to the opponent's end in a jiffy.

While Kielstad kills the penalty on the ice, my sight wanders over to the zamboni door. Alumni surround the corner of the boards. Ben's in his posse of friends from Camp Kelmo. Blain's there, as well as another two guys I don't know the names of. And perfect timing, just as if I should study it as a sign from the spiritual world, Danny pops through the game doors and passes Ben to the zamboni room. Ben doesn't hesitate. He locks his focus on the game in front of him.

Two sticks smack against each other on the ice. Everyone from the student section ducks under their arms. A bulky projectile bullets me in the side of my head. My hand flinches up to the spot. Parents and students gasp as they all stare at me, even the players and my mother draw their attention to me.

"Liam," Barrett says. "You okay?"

A hockey puck spins and flattens on the floor by my feet. "Yeah," says I. "I think so." I grab the puck and sauce it onto the ice. Everyone applauds and cheers for me with my tough recovery, but that doesn't help with the headache that beats in my head.

The periods soar by in the rambunctious rivalry game. Kielstad surprisingly wins 3-2. I believe Thomas is to thank for that. Without a great goaltender, the team could be down by a lot more. As long as those young forwards can score goals, this may be a good year for Kielstad. If they could go to state, that would be best for them. Mom would have an awesome opportunity, and she'd have to take me and Barrett along.

Barrett and I let Thrasher lead the way to the concessions area. We're huddled up in a tight squeeze with the rest of the supporting parents and students, waiting for the players to exit the excruciating long hallway. Eyes do attract to the hallway's

7

entrance, but it's not the kids I'm wanting to see. Ben and his friends act like they own this place. Like seriously, they could have used the walkway on the bleachers like the rest of us versus using the back hallway. He just wants the attention on him as the amazing alumni.

His fishiness passes us in the lobby. I release the air that I held in my lungs. In the back by the Library of Skates is the maintenance room. Barrett probably demands the room torn apart. One picture sticks in his mind like syrup to skin. Shawn's bloodshed, his disappearance, all with one explanation of Coach Kipp's deadly corpse bounded at the arena.

Taps on my shoulder twists my direction in a one-eighty. A tall, thick man towers over me and the boys. He's dressed in puffy winter gear. He takes his cap off and lowers it to his side. The three yellow letters on his black cap glow brighter than the sun.

This man's an investigator.

WARNING

In a packed room full of hockey parents and high school students, the investigator pulls me aside from the bunch, exposing me like a red canoe on blue waters. I'm hoping nobody noticed his cap, cause other than that, he matches the rest of the bunch with his winter carnival on. It's not a bad thing to overdress during the winter, especially since vehicles can never be trusted. They'll break down on you, or even worse, the keys are locked in the car. Only did that twice in my life; one moment was in the high school parking lot, and the other at the pool when I worked there. My lifeguard certification expired, and I'm not fond of swimming. No more lifeguarding for me, which is okay because I never find it satisfying to touch the deep end of the pool. The deep water spikes my anxiety.

Barrett and Thrasher amuse my situation while the investigator talks to me by the excruciating long hallway, "How are you, Liam?"

My toes lift my heels off the ground as my eyes peek behind his shoulders. Hopefully, mom won't notice what's happening here. It's too much to explain to an investigator already. "Who are you? What do you want?"

"You can call me Investigator." He leans his lips into my ears. "I don't give out my name, son."

"Every investigator has a name," says I.

"We have a lot of stupid investigators out there in the world of crime. Why would you want to give your name up to a world full of killers?"

"So, you can gain their trust," says I. "Pretty simple." He probably doesn't want to speak of this nuisance anymore. "I'd like to go back to my friends now." Before my back faces him, he grabs me by the shoulders.

"We have unfinished business," he says.

The boys' voices echo in the excruciating long hallway. Investigator releases his grip from my shoulders. He stares me down as I make my way back to Barrett and Thrasher. While we stand in the lobby and wait for our friends from the locker room, my headache from the hockey puck bounces in my head again. It's hard to listen to all the voices in the room. A group of hockey dads burst into laughter, ringing my ears with piercing stabs.

Barrett finds my hand over one of my ears. "Are you okay?" he says. "Your head still hurt?"

"It does," says I. "It's not bleeding, is it?"

"Your head?" Barrett says. "Not that I can see."

"I don't see any blood," Thrasher adds. He catches the

Dorcha boys carrying their bags to the double set of french doors. "Alright, guys. I should probably talk to some of my guys and then head out." Me and Barrett bump fists with him before he wanders away in the cozy crowd.

"That guy you talked to?" Barrett says.

"He was an investigator," says I. "You know what for."

"He's bringing us into it right now? C'mon. It's almost Christmas break. This happened during the fricken summer."

"I don't know what he wants, but we need to figure out how to shut this place down. We have to kill The Barn."

"Wouldn't that mean tearing it down?" Barrett asks. "We'd never get away with something like that."

"I hope not," says I. "There has to be another way."

"Can't we just leave this place and let it live in peace?"

"You and I both know it's gonna fire back up at some point. Once it has blood to feed off of, it's going to wake up, and it has what it needs already."

"What is it waiting for?" Barrett rouses an interesting question. I'm not sure what it's waiting for. Maybe for a lighter audience, trying to keep its identity hidden in its cave. Or maybe The Barn runs on some sort of clock where only time can tell. But with all the strange events today during the game, I'm suspicious something's up.

Jake, Charlie, and Thomas exit the excruciating long hallway. "Let's talk to Kiv afterwards. He's the manager here. He can help us out."

"Okay," Barrett says. My arms urge the temptations for hugs

11

when the boys arrive. It's been a while since we've been connected in the arena together. Sparks shock inside of our hearts with an electric current flowing between our connections.

"Great game out there," says I.

"It's great to see you again," Thomas says.

"Yeah," Jake says. "Seriously great."

"How's school going?" Charlie asks.

"It's a dandy time of doing homework and more homework," says I. I feel as if that's an appropriate answer. Barrett stands in silence. "Oh, my bad. Guys, this is Barrett. We met at camp, and now, he's living with me."

"We should have a sleep over at your house," Charlie says.

"Dude," Jake says. "That would be dope. The four of us could chel all night."

"Well," says I. I consider the opportunity on an anxious, painful night.

"Please!" Jake and Charlie say in sync.

"Fine. I'll ask my mom," says I.

"Yay!" the guys cheer.

Charlie points to the hallway. "There's Jenny now." Charlie and Jake run over to my mom and bring her to a halt. "Can we sleep over tonight, Jenny?"

"After burning the Dragons in their own flames, I believe we should celebrate," mom says. "How bout we meet at Carbone's? Then you boys can stay the night."

Jake and Charlie run back to me, Thomas, and Barrett. "She said yes!"

Mom drives me, Thomas, and Barrett to Carbone's Pizzeria. Once Charlie dropped his car off at his house, him and Jake carpooled together in Jake's car. We huddle in our group in front of the waiting podium for seating. It's a busy night near the holidays. Carbone's is decked out in Christmas lights; they even have a Christmas tree decorated by the arcade machines.

The waiter takes us over to a high-top table near a window. I end up closing the blinds to block out the falling snow in the dark. It makes the place feel cozier, almost like being bundled up in a bunch of blankets while wearing a hoodie in bed. The waiter writes our orders down on a notepad and leaves for our drinks.

Root beer bottles clank on our coasters. The bottle of liquified root bark reminds me of someone. There's been a time and a place in this restaurant with him. With a little more thought, this was the exact same table we sat in the midst of summer. After all the starvation we fought through, this was the table of feasting.

Ash. I wonder how the Army's treating him.

GREENHOUSE

The light flushes out as Ash and his trainees are locked in a concrete shed. He's along the wall, cramped in the middle of suited soldiers. Ash's vision hazes in a gas mask. The drill sergeant burns a substance on a small heater. Smoke tails off the substance and whirls into the air. The recruits lose all train of thought while amused with the chemical concoction. Ash on the other hand bounces his foot off the floor. His back flattens against the wall, and his shoulders squeeze into his chest while he's trapped between other recruits. Torsha, one of his bunkmates, smiles at him in excitement from across the room. And Quinone, another one of his bunkmates, bulges his eyes to the rising smoke. Ash understands the abundance of emotions; he's been in this state before, thanks to his past.

With one deep breath in, and one deep breath out, Ash prepares himself for the thing he's been most anxious about. The drill sergeant steps away from the burning chemicals and faces her trainees. "Soldiers," she says. "Remember, it's important to stay calm. Control your breath. Move your head slowly from side to side. Look at the person next to you."

Ash moves his head in slow motion. Laughter builds in his head while he tries to joke about the twisting pigeon heads around the room. It's his medicine to laugh the anxiety out, but of course, don't let the humor release itself in the fort. Sergeants will pay you for releasing the inner child.

"Now graciously move your head up and down," the drill sergeant says. She studies the soldiers, tracking their focus. Ash locks eyes with her as she confronts him. "What are you looking at, soldier?"

"Sorry, sergeant," he says. The ceiling attracts his eyes, concrete being his only current friend in the room. With the recruits having to focus on themselves, Ash can't get the support from his bunk buddies. Using the concrete ceiling lets him paint his imagination on the plain canvas, splashing the thoughts of family and home. He hasn't been able to speak with them for some time now, but there's a lot of time left.

"High knees," the drill sergeant orders. "Let's go!" Ash drives his knees high in the cramped line of soldiers. Hockey warmups always had high knees. The comfort of anything that thrives from home lightens the depression Ash is forced to live with. As a member of the Army, he needs to get used to living away from home.

"Settle down, soldiers," she says. "Take a deep breath, hold that breath in, then slide your mask off of your face." Ash pops the gas mask off of his face. His eyes squeeze shut, along with his mouth. It's tougher holding the breath in the air than it is in water. At least the water tempts to trap the air inside a person's lungs, rather than an animal desperate for the oxygen that touches their lips. "Put your masks back on. Make sure they're on before you breathe in." Once Ash plops and locks the mask back on, he drinks all the air he can.

The recruits regain their strength. The drill sergeant gives the last set of instructions. Ash pulls his gas mask off, exposing his lungs to the tear gas that floods the room. His next step is to buckle his combat helmet. During the roughest of experiences, soldiers still have to maintain their duties, staying on task and finishing the mission.

Ash chokes on the tear gas, coughing the hairs and muck clogging his throat. His eyes bubble up in tears. Saliva drools from his lips, gooping all the way down to his boots. The drill sergeant is yelling something in the room, but Ash can only think of his survival. He wants out.

They're all ordered to place their hands on the person's shoulders in front of them. Finally, a glimpse of light flashes inside the concrete shed. The train of soldiers pulls out of the station as Ash escapes into the lush wilderness full of trees, flowers, and oxygen.

"Flap your eagle wings!" the drills sergeant yells. Ash disconnects from the train and flaps his wings, stumbling backwards. "I said an eagle, not a hummingbird." Ash follows orders, opening his eyes so he can somewhat see what's in front of him. It's more like blobs of colors, dizzying his mind into confusion, but he finds the line of soldiers again and continues chugging along.

After the soldiers relieve themselves from the gas chamber, they eat lunch on the warm grass. Thin silver bags hold Ash's lunch. He tears the first bag open which contains a peanut butter and jelly sandwich. His teeth chew in the gushy bread and crunch upon the nuts inside. Another silver pouch contains lasagna, one of his favorites back home. Anything Italian the day before a big game would suit his stomach. And saving the best for last, Ash bolts for the dessert pouch, settling his stomach with a lemon poppyseed pound cake. It's one of the best meals Ash has had at camp here.

"That cake looked marvelous," Torsha says. She digs into her dessert pouch and pulls out a cherry pastry. "Guess this'll have to do for now."

"I got a snickerdoodle cookie," Quinone says.

"Oh!" Torsha says with joy. "Can we swap?"

"I don't know," he says. "Maybe I should taunt you with it. What do you think Ash?"

"I'd be careful, Quinone," Ash says. "She's stealthy. She'll get ya back if you mess with her."

"Heck yeah, Ash," Torsha says. "You should listen to him."

"I guess we can swap then," Quinone says. "At least I'll have some cherry in mine now. I can use the fruit."

After lunch, the crew starts their gun training. Ash shot guns in the past, hunting for pheasant and geese back in Minnesota, but he's never been to a firing range where he impales the wooden head of a human being. Rifle marksmanship. Red dot sights are connected to the rifles while the soldiers work on hitting their targets accurately. Ash's rifle rebounds off of his shoulder with every bullet bursting through the barrel. Sure, it's easy for him to shoot a plank of wood, but Ash can't imagine his first human target. War will say its welcomes at some point in his life.

While working in the red and orange dirt of the firing range all afternoon, Ash and his bunkmates plunge into their cots. Quinone falls asleep faster than the camp teaches them, controlling their breathing and thoughts, but Ash and Torsha busy themselves. Torsha's productive, writing in her daily journal, but Ash is stuck in the slush. Thoughts from the firing range of killing a human being melt into his memories, mixing up the bad and the unthinkable. He envisions the cemetery in Kielstad, with the friends he'd lost. Then he finds the rink with the ice patiently waiting for his skates to carve up. The fans rile up in the stands as his teammates pop on the ice. His best friend is there too.

Ash spots Torsha on the side of his eye, glancing at him. Maybe he's made his emotions too noticeable. He understands why she's looking at him. He knows she's either concerned for him or she's going through the exact same emotions. Bagged up.

Homesick.

FARMHOUSE

A crustiness builds in my eyes. Staring at the television all night, gaming on chel with the guys, I'm dozing off to another dimension. Thomas and Charlie tap buttons on the controller, satisfying my ears with calm clicks. Jake is entertained with the third period in the game. Barrett on the other hand fell asleep about an hour ago. I'm still up for that only reason. Part of me wants to trust the boys, but I can't take chances with anybody. They'd probably pull some strings, picking a prank from a hat to see what they'd have to do to us silent sleepers. I know they wouldn't do anything like that, but boys will be boys without second thought every once in a while.

My eyes turn into drapes, falling over my eyes while the light casts through. With the lights dancing through my closed eyelids, the clicks from the buttons and joysticks, the joy and disappointment from the guys; it all conjures up a dream. My skates are tied on my feet, and my helmet holds the cage against my foggy breath. My hockey stick glues to my gloved hands. Fans from the stands roar with ambition as players soar passed me on the ice like concords. In the middle of The Barn, I stand, my blades frozen in the ice. My feet, they can't move. My skates are locked into the cold ice. All the skaters leave me high to cherry-pick. The rest of them play the puck down low. Over on the bench, Coach Kipp studies the ice. He can clearly see four Kielstad players out on the ice, but he can't see me. When I try to yell at him, that I'm here on the ice where I'm supposed to be, he doesn't budge. He sends another guy onto the ice to play. Behind me, the fans' joy burns like a wildfire. They all jump from their seats, applauding a recent goal for the Kielstad Knights. No one notices I'm standing here. Stuck.

A flash of light jolts me from my blankets. Over by my windows, the morning sun rises. The soft ambient sound of heat blowing through the vents comforts my winter warmth. If only I had Christmas lights in my room, along the walls, that would be the star on top of the tree. The boys slumber beside me in their blanket cocoons. Usually, I don't end up waking this early in the morning, but a wave of stress settles in my stomach. It has nothing to do with me needing food. The pizza packed me up last night, but I guess it is breakfast time. One thought floats into my mind though. There's something Barrett and I forgot to do the other night. With the investigator stomping the snow into The Barn, and the strange phenomena at the game, and the deaths rising from the past, it lingers around me like backwash swimming around in my beverages.

We need to do some homework. Research. Even though me and Barrett are in school, we have to do work of our own. Gross. We're in the developmental stages of becoming wrinkly, wonky wombats (I guess they're called adults). Age is just a number. Since I believe in the afterlife, I'm attached to the faith of unlimited soul life. So, assuming I have eighty years left, that's actually not too long. That number's not even in the triple digits. We're all children of this Earth, and it's best to envision it like that. Even adults like to play like kids; running through the rain, going out to the movies, playing on the playground, coloring with chalk. Age is just a scientific number. I don't count Earth's revolution by years, I count them with memorable moments. Might as well make the best moments you can.

Our first move is to dig some arti-facts about The Barn. We need to learn the history behind the rink if we're going to get anywhere close to killing it. If we can't understand how this monster was born, we'll be stepping in quicksand. We'd all sink into the ground pretty fast. But currently, only Barrett and I were up for this. Until we find out what we're getting ourselves into, it's just going to be the two of us. Most of the guys will be busy with Christmas break around the corner.

My bedroom door creaks open. Mom pokes her head in, finding me as the only conscious being in the room. My nose picks up a sweet scent. Breakfast must be ready for us.

"Good morning," mom whispers.

"Mornin," says I. "Did you bake something for breakfast?"

"Yes, I did," she says. "The monkey bread is cooling off on

the table. You should try to wake your guys up before it's noon."

"What time is it?" I ask.

"It's nine right now," she says, "but my instincts bet those boys will want to sleep in till the snow melts."

And with that, I'm cautiously waking the boys from their comfy cocoons. I try to pull Thomas' blanket off of him, but he rips it loose from my grip. He's a cranky crow in the morning. Don't wanna mess with that bed head of his. Eventually, the other boys annoy him enough to come stampeding down the steps. We all nestle into our nests around the dining table, digging into the monkey bread. Washing the cinnamon down with eggnog is the best cleansing in the world, although, it's quite a cold drink for the wintertime.

After breakfast, Charlie, Jake, and Thomas head out. Jake pulls out of the driveway with them on board. The tires squeak through the fresh snow that coated our driveway in a heaping one foot. At least it's a snowy winter this year. The seasons like to play leapfrog in Minnesota, jumping from one climate to the next. It could be a tropical rainforest tomorrow, then a severe freeze warning the next morning. It's kind of nice having a bipolar climate though. It makes for beautiful sights. I've always wanted to stare into the Northern Lights, but down in Kielstad, the lights from the cities create enough pollution where we can't even see the swirling milk in our own galaxy.

Barrett and I double check our schoolwork, affirming that we don't have homework due the following day. Since our homework is complete, we decide to drive to The Barn to begin our research.

I told mom we were gonna play on the outdoor rink by The Barn, but of course, whenever I want to play out there (or use it as an excuse), there's snow loaded on top of it. Mom questioned it, but I came up with the thought that we'd just shoot in the dryland room. I'm not a lenient liar, but mom's easy to trick.

Out front, Danny's car is nowhere to be found. This can only mean Kiv is on shift. We kick the snow into The Barn. Mini mites practice on the ice, pretty typical for a weekend morning. Most mites don't complain about the morning practices either. They're strange creatures. I've never questioned that. Over in the Library of Skates, the skate sharpener sparks a set of blades. Barrett and I wait in the chairs by the shelves of skates.

The skate sharpener quiets. Kiv exits with a pair of skates, handing them to a man outside of the door. Then, he approaches us. "What's up, boys?" he asks. "Need a skate sharpenin?"

"Actually," says I. "No. We were wondering if you could help us out with something."

"What do you need help with?" he asks.

"We'd like to know some history behind The Barn," says I.

"What kind of history are you looking for?" he asks.

"Well, for starters, I think it'd be nice to know who built this place," says I. Kiv chuckles. "What?" I whisper to Barrett, "Was it something I said?" Barrett shakes his head no.

"This barn has been here for decades," Kiv says. "The man's dead. History's buried in the dirt."

"Who's the man?" says I.

"Mr. Muckens," he says. "The Muckens owned this land way

back in the sixties. Used to be their dairy farm. And this barn, this was the dairy house. They stored cows here sometimes during the winter, protected them from the storms."

"I thought farmers just left them to survive out in the storm," says I. "You know, sleep in the snow and breathe in the cold."

"You'd be right," Kiv says, "but I believe the wife of The Barn cared for the cows in her own way." Kiv pauses. "I'm sorry, why do you guys want to know this stuff again?" My tongue hangs out to dry like clothes on a linen line.

Barrett responds, "I'm writing a research paper for history class. I thought I could do it on The Barn."

"Interesting history class," Kiv says. "Why's he asking all the questions for you then?" His finger points to me.

"He's better at asking questions than me," Barrett says.

"Well, as much as I wish I could help ya more, that's all I got on the table," Kiv says.

"You were great help," says I. "Do you know any living relatives of the Muckens family we could speak to?"

"I think Mr. Muckens' son works at the grocery store in town," he says. "I can't be sure though. Got a lot on my mind." Kiv accidently knocks down a stack of paperwork onto the floor. His fist pounds the desk. "I think you boys better duck out. I got a lot of work to do."

"Okay," says I. I leave the room.

"Thanks for your time," Barrett says. He catches up to me.

We leave The Barn, stomping the snow off of our shoes and onto the floor mats of my SUV. I crank the key in the ignition, boosting the engine for heat.

"What now?" Barrett asks.

"We gotta go to the grocery store," says I. "If he works there, maybe he can give us the answers were looking for."

Stalking a snowplow on the roads, we arrive to the grocery store on the other side of town. It's more on the outskirts of the new-development homes in Kielstad. Just like any other grocery store in a small town, the prices here rocket to the moon. Me and Barrett shuffle through the snow to the front doors of Schnickels.

Time to search the store for the Muckens man.

DEAD & DAIRY

Only a small chunk of locals shop in the early morning at Schnickels. Grocery shopping is usually a noon or evening activity around here. There's rarely anyone in line at the checkout stands. One out of three of the workers is actually scanning goods for an elderly couple. Other than that, it's pretty chillaxed up front. In the entrance, sugary sweets tempt me and Barrett. Such a strategic way to get children's attention. They'll pull upon their parents' arms to do anything for those goodies. One thing that's ironic, we're not here for actual groceries. Of course, I can go for some saltwater taffy, or even some chocolate malt rounds, but sliding the temptations back to their shelves is best for me. We have an objective anyways. Kiv said Mr. Muckens works here, the son of the man who owned The Barn on his belated farm.

Not starting at a point of interest, Barrett and I stroll in between the checkout stands and aisle fronts. We pass the aisles that hold canned goods, pasta supplies, breakfast food, candy, beverages, bread, chips, and other grocery needs. Back at the cashiers, I guess we could have asked them where this Muckens man was, but my anxiety didn't want to since they were more out in the open. Drawing attention to myself is the last resort.

The aisle passages convert into cold, stained buses. Each fridge aisle has fogged up glass doors, smudging the view to all the pizzas and pies and ice cream treats inside. As if it wasn't cold enough outside, Barrett and I sway away from the drifting freeze. The store spaces out in front of us. Wooden stands hold boxes of donuts and bread rolls, right in front of the bakery. The bakery's tucked onto our left. An older lady with soft crinkles packs a cake into its plastic home. She's shorter than us. While she finishes her packaging on the cake, her green eyes spot us moving up to the cash register. "I'll be right there, honey," she says. Her hands vibrate while sticking the packaging label on the plastic. Finally, she finishes her shaky situation. "What can I do for ya, two lads?"

"We were wondering if you could help us," says I.

"What baking questions do ya have for me?" she asks.

"Actually, we didn't have questions about baking," says I.

"Oh, silly me," she says. "I should know better. It's only the ol folks that asks those questions around here. You two have smooth faces, which can only mean you're here for the frosted treats."

"No," says I. "We don't want any food."

"We ate breakfast already," Barrett says.

"Oh, silly me," she says. "I think you're searching for the liquor store. Yes, that's it. You continue the way you were going, and to the left will be the coffee shop, and on the right of the gas station shop are the sliding doors to the liquor store." Barrett and I glue to the ground. We can't whip out words. "I totally understand how tough it is to find your way around this maze. Ya know, I used to work on a ship for the Navy in World War II."

"No way," Barrett says. "So, your ship survived?"

"Of course, it did," she answers. "We had the best men and women on board. But dang my doodle, that ship was a sweet mess. There were tunnels of pipes and steel that twisted and cranked in all sorts of directions. After some time though, I finally memorized a path from my bouncy bed to the kitchen."

"You cooked on the ship too?" Barrett asks.

"That's right, honey," she says. "The soldiers loved my food so much, they called me Empress Esla. Oh, silly me. I didn't give you boys my name. I'm Ms. Esla."

"Nice to meet you, Ms. Esla," says I. "Do you know a Muckens man?"

"A Muckens man?" she says. Her eyes search the ceiling lights above. "Are you looking for Chuckle?"

"Chuckle who?" I ask.

"Chuckle Muckens," she says. "I believe that's the man you're looking for."

"Yes," says I. "Does he work here?"

"Mm hmm," she says. "He's the butcher in the back. He runs the meat counter."

"Thank you," says I. Barrett and I will have to walk through the thriving veggies to get to the back of the store, that's where the

28

butcher shop is.

"Wait," Ms. Esla says. One of her pointer fingers shakes at us. "You two better be careful. Chuckle doesn't like the annoyance children bring these days. He's like an old lady on Main Street, yelling at kids to step off the grass."

"Aren't you an old lady?" Barrett asks.

I slap his arm. "Barrett!" says I.

"No worries, honey," Ms. Esla says. "I may be old, but I still have my swing in me." She swings into a dance in the bakery. Her dancing takes her over to unwrapped breads. This is our gateway to break from the bakery.

On our wanderlust journey through the veggies, a rainstorm rumbles on the green food. A rainforest for the flies perhaps. They can fly through the trees of celery and kale and carrots and chords while in the midst of a mist. The machine also crackles with thunder when it bursts on. Pretty neat for a small store in Kielstad.

Reaching the back of the store, a couple of freezer aisles hold meats, hinting our way to the butcher shop. No customers push carts around the deep freezers nor the dairy products far down in the aisle. The butcher shop sits right in the back of the store, centered with the long submarine freezer. A buff man with gorilla muscles and a chubby face slams a butcher's knife into a slab of messy meat. I'm not a big fan of meat. It's all guts and intestines.

Plodding to the counter, the big buff man doesn't inch an eye on us. "Are you Mr. Muckens?" I ask. He smacks the butcher's knife in the meat. "Mr. Muckens."

He sticks the knife into the meat, grabs a brown-stained towel and wipes the slob from his fingers. "What do you want?"

"We were wondering if you could tell us about The Barn," says I. "The history behind your father's farm."

"My father's dead," Mr. Muckens says.

"I understand it's hard," says I, "but we need your help." His back turns to us. He doesn't want to breathe another word about this. "The Barn killed three of my friends. It would be generous if you could show some support."

Mr. Muckens' head angles back to us, but his eyes stare into the floor. "Thanks to Pa, I've been butchering for forty years now. He taught me how to cut up a pig, milk a cow, chop a chicken. Ma never wanted to splatter the blood. While she gardened our crops, Pa forced me to slaughter them when I was six. I had the muscles, just not the strength. Every month, I'd find myself drenched in tears, but all those years of butchering them, I've gotten used to it. A storm of locusts broke out one season, eating all our crops away, but they also sickened our livestock. Pa was pissed. We didn't have the money to spare in that chaos. So, he tried to invent something that'd bring them back to life."

"How can you bring a dead cow back to life?" says I.

"Fresh blood, a beating heart," Mr. Muckens says. "Ma wanted to leave the farm for financial sakes."

"Did she leave you behind?" I ask.

"No," Mr. Muckens says. "Pa put a bullet in her brain." A fire erupts in my heart. Murder.

"Was he arrested?" Barrett asks.

"No," Mr. Muckens says. "She was considered missing."

"What did he do with her then?" says I.

"Pa took Ma's healthy heart, implanted it in a dead pig, then took her blood and swapped it with the pigs. All I remember seeing in that barn were a lot of cords." Mr. Muckens grabs a new slab of meat and continues cutting.

"Mr. Muckens," says I. "The Barn. Your father's contraption of cords. It's still alive."

"A contraption doesn't have a life of its own," he says.

"No," says I, "but your father does."

The butcher knife points directly at my face. "What are you saying, boy?"

"The Barn is still alive," says I. "Maybe your father's spirit still lingers there."

"I want you out of here," Mr. Muckens says. "Now."

"Wait," says I. "Did he leave you behind with anything? There has to be a way we can shut it down."

"Shut it down?" he says.

"Please, Mr. Muckens," says I. "I can't lose anyone else."

He questions it. "I remember my Pa leaving behind a trail of puzzle pieces."

"Puzzle pieces?" I ask.

"Four letters," he says. "H-E-L-L." It takes me seconds before déjà vu kicks in. "Did ya know plants can feel things? Well, the dead can feel things too. While Pa was crazy, I remember finding an etch in our small shed's wall. He carved out four letters out from that drabby wood. Later on, that day, he told me about them. He told me how he's gonna hide them. He gave me the starting spot to the puzzle, but I never cared."

"Where is it?" says I.

"Before I tell you anymore, we need to make a deal," he says.

"What kind of deal?" says I.

"You have to buy meat," he says.

Barrett and I think it over, but it's a fair deal. "Deal," says I.

Mr. Muckens slams a thing of meat onto the counter. Barrett pulls out cash. He's generous to pay for the food I won't eat. Again, I don't like a lot of meat. Pepperoni's the only meat I'll ever be able to satisfy on my taste buds. Mr. Muckens spills the beans on the starting spot of this four-letter puzzle.

The Box. It's a community center in the neighboring town of Le Seuer. What's even weirder is that he says his father hid the four-letters in hockey arenas around our state of Minnesota. Why would he hide them in hockey arenas? Anyways, Barrett and I have to find something in The Box.

We can't find our treasure without its map.

THE BOX

Luggage packs the trunk of my vehicle. Mother slides in tupperware full of treats and sandwiches for the long trip. She doesn't know what Barrett and I are up to, but we told her we were gonna travel up north to an oasis on Lake Superior. While me and Barrett search the state on a huge scavenger hunt for four letters that spell an anonymous word, mom will busy herself into believing were swimming in a hotel's indoor waterpark. Now, this mission can only succeed if we discover this mystery object. Muckens said that we need this thing in order for the letters to lead us to them. The starting point of this hunt was quite flat and bland when Muckens explained it to us. This object hides inside of the community center in Le Seuer. The Box. That's our first rendezvous, and we have to break The Box in order to receive the precious prize.

It's quite cold outside. Temp's around zero-degrees fahrenheit this morning. The day's closing in on noon in a couple of hours. Hopefully, we'll be on the potholed freeways by then.

Mom closes the trunk door while me and Barrett buckle up in my heated SUV. "Alright," she says. "I don't know what the weather's gonna be like. The roads are icy today though. Drive very slowly. Use four-wheel drive."

"Sounds good," says I.

"Watch out for deer too," she adds.

"Yep," says I.

"Oh, don't forget to call me when you get there," she adds to the adds that she already added.

"Okay, mom," says I.

"Okay," she says. "Love you."

Ugh. "Love you too."

"Bye, mom," Barrett says.

"Bye, Barrett," she says to him. "Keep an eye on him."

"Will do," Barrett says.

After a decade in the driveway, the tires roll off my gravel driveway and onto the icy country road. Four-wheel drive isn't doing much help. The ice takes my steering wheel, shaking it into a washing machine. The back of the car slides on the ice, heading for the ditch. In front, a truck appears on top of the nearby hill. They get a free thrill, watching the front of my car slip along the yellow lines. Whatever shall happen, I'm not supposed to hit the brakes while sliding. It makes it worse. Just go with the flow and casually slow so you don't blow and need a tow. Self-explanatory.

Le Sueur's one of the odd ball towns in the state, no one really knows about it. It's slowly growing into a bigger town as the metro expands, but I still see it as a farmer's field. There's not much to do out there if you don't have a snowmobile. But the town has a very special community center. I've practiced on The Box's rink before. It's quite a different rink to play in. First thing that's weird about it is that there's a second floor for the bleachers that sits above the benches, parents can easily perch their heads over the rails and yell at us if they cared to do so. There was also a sketchy dryland area surrounded in a baseball-like netting, protecting the walls and patrons from flying pucks. Quality with the ice is pretty good, but the air was so musty and dark in the past. I'm sure it still is. The Box is old. Outdated swimming pool, a musty arena, but it does have a fresh basketball court.

A dead raccoon sleeps in the middle of the icy road. Doing so gently, I curve around the mushed-up roadkill. If the roads stay like popsicles the entire drive, this'll be the longest day of anxiety. Usually roadkill on a drive brings bad luck. Now's not the time. There'll be days where buffets of roadkill steam in the ditch's snow, and I get delusional about it. Dad though, he'd remind me by saying, "one only confuses themself if they made the mold." And I take his advice for granted, every day. Positive thoughts and keeping my head held high pulls in the good.

After a half-hour drive on the crooked country roads, Barrett and I arrive at The Box. I park in front of the snow-covered baseball field. I can already hear the chain-linked fence shaking in the winter wind. The roof over the baseball stands matches the color of The Box's roof. A faded, dark green. The whole building is literally a cement box. No wonder where its nickname thrived from. We hop out of my SUV, scanning around the vacant village. Although, there are two cars in the puny parking lot.

We walk the sidewalk past the baseball stadium and find the doors to The Box. Heat hovers in the entrance. The ceiling almost touches the tip of my hat's beanie. Over on the left, Barrett twists around to a lady working in the front desk, which is also a concession stand for the front of the center. It's a small stand. There's candy and snacks, just not a lot of room.

"Can I help you folks out?" she asks.

"We wanted to check this place out," says I.

"Not a problem," she says. "In the middle of the long hall, right in front of the doors you just walked through, is the swimming pool and basketball court. Further down the hall, it turns into a T-way. On the right is a gym, which is closed today, and on the left, you'll get to two doors that lead to the hockey rink."

"Thank you," says I.

"No problem," she says. She watches us move to the long skinny hallway as we disappear around the corner. The cement cinderblock walls lead us to two doors. One door is flushed on the wall to our left, the basketball court. On the right, a mini, dark hall pokes into the swimming pool. The chlorine floats under the door, bringing back memories from the pool back in Kielstad. Lots of work, lots of pathetic patrons, but it was a good learning experience, working at the edge of the waters and learning its danger. The danger it contains, taking away innocent lives of children. Only a lifeguard could have saved those kids. Only if I was there for him.

"Where do we even start?" Barrett says.

"Well, the place is called The Box for a reason," says I. "It's needing to be opened."

"Like a Christmas gift," he says.

"Or a safe," says I.

"Maybe there's a safe at the front desk," he says.

"Could be, but then we need the code. Let's just take a look around this place for a while like we said."

Our first destination is the bright basketball court. It smells fresh with slick wooden floors. There's no room for an audience nor a team. The court's for physical fitness uses only. The lights hang on the wooden-beamed ceiling, but they're not doing any good use while the light from outside glows through the windows above the two emergency exits. In between the doors and the windows is an air vent dividing them from each other. A logo of cheese splats on middle court. The Cheese Gallery. A shop in town. Maybe it's a clue. The logo prints on the blue protective mats under the basketball hoops too.

With nothing of interest in the basketball court, Barrett and I slide across the hall to the swimming pool. The smell of chlorine makes me happy. It produces the child inside of me. I remember swimming here back in middle school on a field trip. A couple hundred of us swam, skated, and dunked that day. I did a little bit of everything, and of course, I brought my own pair of skates. It's nice to show-off once in a while, makes me proud and noticed.

A tan paints the wall and floor tiles. The only color that

splashes out in this room is the blue water, a blue Pepsi clock, a tropical blue stripe running along the wall with tropical fish painted over it, and the blue tiles that outline the pool's caution zone. Other than that, the whole place is tan. Above the shallow end of the pool where the Pepsi clock ticks are windows into a viewing room. That's where us middle-school dwellers had lunch that day. This memory fogs in my mind, not something I really remembered till now. On top of the ceiling are the same wooden beams. No other sign of cheese in this room.

We leave the swimming pool and move forth down the long skinny hall. The T-way. It flows left and right. To the right are a couple of vending machines, standing by two closed doors. Beside me on the left is the bigger concession stand. It's arranged as if it's a corner-lot house; one gate in the long skinny hallway, and the other gate facing the way to the hockey rink.

Darkness floats back here. There are no windows inviting the light in. Empty benches rest on the floor. The Box seems abandoned. Barrett marches down to the left. Further down on the right, two doors enter into the lower level of the arena, but to get to the bleachers, we must continue forth and twist up the curvy steps. The staircase is separated into its own little box at the end of the hall. Two doors can technically split the stairs from the small hall, but they're always opened.

Reaching the top, we open the doors to the quiet arena. Everything's still. Not a gust of wind whooshes inside the rectangle room. Wooden supports keep the flat, wooden ceiling high. Division of bleachers line along the metal rails. Under the huge concrete floor where we stand are the locker rooms. Barrett and I stroll along the top and scan the room for any more hints. At the end of the bleachers are the tangled baseball nets. Such a sketchy place to shoot pucks at a net. Over on the far side of the ice, near the player's benches, is another Pepsi clock. An American Flag stalls on the wall, waiting for its National Anthem. One thing pops out to me in this room. The town's team bolds in blue on the wall.

"Barrett," says I. "I think we've found it."

"Bulldogs," he says. "Brilliant."

"If we're right about this, it has to be a code to a safe."

"Let's go find that safe then," he says.

Leaving the arena, we approach the front desk again, after a long walk in the skinny hallway. The lady vanished. She isn't in sight. I peek through the plastic which protects the desk from a riveting robbery. There's a normal cash register. Candy stacks the bottom shelves in a glass case. In the back is a room full of cabinets. A door props open to the concession stand. Barrett's sneaking inside.

"Barrett!" I whisper. He tiptoes like a ninja into the room. My lips twitch with my anxiety pulling at my veins. Acne's gonna breakout for me after this trip. I just know it. "Please come out."

"Just go look out for me," he says. "Check the hallways. Stall her if ya can."

"This is crazy," I say from under my breath.

I act all innocent in the long skinny hallway. I tuck my hands in my sweatshirt pockets. The beanie on my hat bounces with my quick pace. Peeking into the court and the pool, there's no movement in sight. I continue down the hallway, checking back from time to time for any stalking ghosts. I wish I felt Finn's presence with me when he passed away, but the only thing I felt was a darkness lurking inside of my stomach, and I still do.

At the T-way, I turn right. Two closed doors block my path. Three vending machines stick side-by-side on the wall. One vending machine has all sorts of snacks and candy bars. Another machine contains pop and athletic fuel. And last in line is an old coffee machine. I tap the buttons, attempting to open the vending machine with my magic, but I realize something. Numbers are on the candy machine's buttons, and handwritten letters beneath them. It's here. It has to be. The Box is the vending machine.

Normal vending machines have a combination of a letter and a number for a snack selection, but this machine asks for a four-number code. A four-letter word. Hell doesn't work; no H is present for a letter choice. I thought the code was bulldogs, but it does include two four-letter words. With the keypad only having twelve buttons, there's only twelve letters to work with. Bull surprisingly works. 1-B; 5-U; 2-L; 2-L.

Beep! The machine's green little screen reads two more attempts. Who knows what'll happen if I fail these next two? Dogs. It also functions with the buttons. 7-D; 4-O; 6-G; 9-S.

Beep! Incorrect. One more guess, and I don't have a clue. Barrett pops from around the corner with a hand squeezing his wrist. The front desk lady grasps on to him. "I should have known better than to walk to my car while having two young boys venturing around." My chest blows into an air balloon. I can't release any air out. It's trapped inside. The lady reaches for my hand, but she spots the vending machine's blinking words. "You boys aren't here to rob me, are ya?"

"It's not what it looks like," Barrett says.

"Do you know a man named Mr. Muckens?" says I.

"I knew it," she says. "I knew it all along. Chuckle put you up to this, didn't he?"

"You know him?" says I.

"Of course," she says. "Chuckle swims at our pool every week. He's always snooping around the place for something. He said his father hid something for him here."

"Do you know what it is?" says I.

"I have no clue," she says. "But I always keep an eye out on him. You never know when a person might strike."

"I'm close to cracking the case for him, but I have one more attempt with this password," says I. "Do you know what it could be? It's four letters long. I tried bull and dogs already." As she squints in confusion, I study the number pad again. The letters form in my mind. It works. The word works on the pad, and I've seen it in every room. "I found it." I tap the buttons. 1-B; 2-L; 5-U; 0-E. "It's blue."

The vending machine throws something to the bottom. Pushing my hand through the flap-door, a circular object waits for my handling. I pull it out. Barrett and the lady lean over me. It's a hockey puck compass. A hockey stick points north, but it's not the way I'm facing. It's pointing the way for us, the way to our letters.

"A compass?" Barrett says.

"It leads the way," says I. "We found it, Barrett."

"Blue," the lady says. "Chuckle's mentioned Blue before."

"Blue?" says I.

"I think it was a loved one of his," she says. "No, wait. It was one of his favorite pigs on the farm. It died, and he was so upset. He's always telling me silly stories."

Barrett and I decide to head out, getting out of the lady's hair. It's strange to hear about Blue, but apparently Chuckle Muckens couldn't solve his father's puzzle. Now with the hockey puck compass, we can find the letters in the hockey rinks around the state. But someone turns us into icicles.

The investigator.

REFEREE

An empty coffee house. That's the first. Mornings are sprees for caffeine. The clock is closing in on noon though, but a warm cup of joe does just the trick in the crepuscular cold. It's the perfect cliché rendezvous for Investigator. Although we didn't plan on dining with him, he insisted we did, and here we are. Barrett snugs up in his chair next to the wall. On the other hand, I'm stuck with sitting across from the detective. His cup of coffee cools beside his investigative reports. A cold case. One thing's for certain. We don't have to spill out crap to him, no matter how much he craves it.

My cute cup of cappuccino sets on the mini plate in front of me. Barrett's not a fan of coffee. He's in heaven with his hot chocolate. A classic that can't go wrong. And there's a rule when the fans walk into a hockey rink. Never watch a game without a handwarmer. Handwarmer also meaning something hot. Hot chocolate will do the trick every time.

A tiny sip from my cup burns the roof of my mouth. It's elegant and evil. A place like this in a small town bursts my imagination open. The coffee shop sorta takes me on a journey through the medieval times; royalties sharing a cup of tea, raising their pinkies, and cheering with the cup's gold glass. But this isn't the time for one's mind to twirl away.

"My suspicion rose with the sun this morning," Investigator says. "What were you two doing at the community center? You don't live here."

"We were gonna ask you the same thing," says I. "How were you at the same place at just the right time?"

He raises his eyebrows, takes a sip of his cryptic coffee, then releases the truth. "I didn't want to bother you this morning, but I needed answers. While I was on my way to your house, I spotted a car, an SUV, swerving on black ice between the fields." The truck. The embarrassment I had. He was the one driving the truck over the hill, watching my car slide on the ice. "But when you passed, my adrenaline danced."

"You followed us here," Barrett says.

"More like stalked," says I.

"Welcome to my world," he says. "Not the way I had planned for my day, but I'm bounded to these reports, bounded to you boys."

"Why though?" says I. "The case closed. Our whole team answered all the questions we could that summer."

"Yes, but there are many red flags that haven't been hinted at," he says. "I'm here to fill in those potholes."

"Speaking of potholes, could you fix the ones out on 35?" says I. "It'll be a rough drive for us."

"That's not my job, bud," he says.

"Sorry, I thought you'd just have the connections, working with the state and all," says I.

"I do have the connections, but I'm not here to smoothen your slop," he says. "I'm here to clean it up. Now, where did you say you were going today?"

"We're vacationing in Duluth at a resort," Barrett says.

"Aw," he says. "Two young studs heading to a hotel. All alone. No parents. No supervision."

"Well," says I. "A stalker spies on us. We do have a supervisor after all."

Investigator chuckles. "I only have a few questions to ask. Can you consider 'em?"

"Go ahead," says I. "No promise you'll get an answer."

"Camp Kelmo. Thirty hockey players were selected to train in their off season. These kids graduated high school that year. But when the chaos erupted, the reports calculated that three individuals went missing while one was found at the lake with an arrow sticking out between his eyes. The easiest assumption for the summertime investigation was that Annie Moriz committed suicide after what she had done."

"That's what we assumed too," says I. Barrett nods with agreement. "We felt awful for her son."

"Clayton," he says. "He's recouped with his father now. With Ms. Moriz confirmed as our criminal, it made sense that these

'Hunters' killed your boys. It's a tragedy we didn't discover the other two bodies. Orson and Shawn."

"We know the past," says I. He pauses while my anger relieves itself.

"What drives me nuts isn't what happened that summer but the winter before it," he says. "Two hockey boys from Kielstad die followed by their head coach."

"Yes," says I. "Finn committed suicide cause the others couldn't control themselves."

"Others?" he asks.

I hesitate to say anything, but I'm logged up in his words. There's no turning back. "Our first liners. They were mad at him. After our defeat with the Scythes, they left behind their bruises on his skin and bones."

"Who were the first liners?" he says with interest.

"Look," says I. "I don't understand what they have to do with this. They didn't kill him if that's what you're looking for."

"What I'm looking for is crystal clear water, but all I'm getting is floating fog," he says. "I need answers."

"They're right there in the report," says I. "Come on, Barrett. Let's go. We got a long drive." Me and Barrett push from our seats. While we head for the doors, Investigator opens his lips.

"How did you feel after your liney died?" he says.

I stop and spin around. "Excuse me?"

"Chester," he says. "What was your reaction when you—"

I storm over to him. "You don't get to ask me that."

"It appears I do," he says.

"How do you think I feel about it?" says I. The slobber that drips from my spit answers the question for me. I wipe my mouth with my sleeve. Nothing makes me angrier than a person reaching for my emotions. They're mine for a reason. "Sorry." Me and Barrett exit the coffee shop as the detective drinks his dark coffee.

The sun's up. Cold air lingers upon my goosebumps. Arriving to my SUV, the windshield is coated in a thin layer of frost. Most of it probably produced while our masterminds unraveled The Box. In the back trunk lies my handy dandy scraper. Barrett's eyes glue to my hands as they scrape away the windshield's frosting.

"He can't get answers from us without a lawyer," he says.

"He can try," says I. "He won't get any more from us." I vigorously shove the snow off the top. With Barrett's still stance, I toss the scraper for his side's coating.

"Are you alright?" Barrett says.

I'm fricken pissed off, and I'm stressing over every question, but I can't hurt him with my anger. "I'm fine. Just need to leave."

Barrett crawls under my breath and scrapes his side. He knows I didn't tell the truth, but he isn't going to fight it. "So, where's our first letter at?"

"Not positive," says I. "It's in a hockey rink, but only the hockey puck will show us the way." I hop in the car and pop the glovebox open. The hockey stick in the compass points north. "I'm guessing we'll find the letters in order. Hopefully, Mr. Muckens made this an eco-friendly trip."

Barrett brushes the last of the frosting off the car. We jump inside. I blast the heat in the vents, which'll take twenty centuries to heat up, and roll the wheels onto Le Sueur's Main Street. Our first hockey rink awaits for our arrival.

It's time to put an end to this Hell.

BLAZE

Barrett's hands clasp around the hockey puck compass. The mini stick inside gently moves to the right. The blade points to the right of the freeway, making things simpler for me on the road. Keeping my distance in the right lane of traffic, we steady along our route on 35. Cars blast by in the fast lane. The day's still cold. Nothing has changed with the weather. The sun's starting to float its way to the horizon, and in a few hours, it'll be sunset. Four-thirty is when the sun goes down. Daylight savings drains the energy from the North. It sure keeps things quieter and less hectic. Unlike the South, the heat stirs up all sorts of craziness. Great for the snowbirds to take a trip though. Lying under a palm tree with frozen lemonade sounds like soft, ocean waves to me. But the water only reminds me of Orson. And I can't bear to think about death anymore. The clock just mocks every second of my life. With one tic of a second, death can take any of us. Besides, frozen lakes are paradise. If I need to be patient with warm weather, then

I'll wait for it. The longer winter is, the more hockey I can play. There has to be a way I can continue to play hockey. High school's over, but I'm not too far out of it. No one's ever told me the next steps in my hockey career. I'm not sure where the path is anymore. Where do I hike? Is there a mountain I have to climb? Fog just messes with the vision in front of my eyes. I know there's an answer, I just need help finding it.

"Liam," Barrett says. "I think our turns coming."

He holds the puck compass in front of the car's touch screen. The blade ticks to the right. "Burnsville," says I.

"Huh?" Barrett says.

"Burnsville's arena," says I. "Home of the Blaze."

"You think it's there?" he says.

"Guess we'll see where the compass takes us." My car winks its blinker as I exit off the freeway. Stoplights clutter with cars, but we flow with the green light traffic. We pass through the shopping skirts of Burnsville and fade into a neighborhood. And inside the snowy neighborhood waits the Burnsville Ice Center. There are two ice arenas, and they both contain half-domed roofs. They appear as if they were two Swirl Rolls cut in half and layered upon the cold, powdered snow. The exterior is wood with a lake's wave of brick. Cool design for an ice arena. It was built in 1972, adding to the list of vintage rinks in Minnesota. And the inside still has its classic touch.

I remember playing here for a high school game. It was the first game for my junior year of high school. That was my best year yet. The game opener is always the best, even if it's not our

Barn. This place holds a special place in my heart because of that day. Everything was normal. Everything was good. Everything that I wish for today.

Barrett and I leave the vehicle to sleep in the cold. We bundle up in the freezing breeze and into the blazing arena. Sliding doors open us into the wooden dome of Rink One. A low wood ceiling hovers above us. Stairs climb to our left, leading to the bleachers on this side of the arena. Across the rink are more bleachers, but they're not as big. The penalty and score box also divide the far bleachers. Wooden beams hold the nice wooden ceiling.

"Where do we even start?" Barrett says.

"I'm not sure," says I. My eyes catch seven vending machines behind the stairs. Wandering over to them, I read their code pads. No signs present logical sense with 'em. Further down the hall is Rink Two, but what's inside the hall holds something unique. A fresh wooden trophy case shows off Burnsville's successes. And on the other wall that views outside to the parking lot are photographs of older teams. They stick high above the frosted glass, dating back the runner-ups in 1995.

"How long has this place been here?" Barrett says.

"Quite some time," says I.

"Did you play at this rink?" he says. "We did a little bit."

"Yeah," says I. "In high school, we played here twice."

"It's so strange," he says.

"What's strange?" says I.

"It's like we only play in each other's arenas once, and then we just never come back," he says. He's right, unless we had another year of high school hockey. I'm always telling myself that. If I could have one more year, maybe things could have lightened up. Now, I'm lost in a blizzard, not knowing which direction to go.

"Barrett," says I. "Let me see the compass for a sec." When he hands it over, it appears the blade is still pointing the direction to something. The stick points to Rink One. "It points over here."

And just like the freeways, we slide under the overpass of the walkway to the bleachers. Our hearts melt inside the huge wooden cathedral. This ice rink is beautiful. The wood paints the arena in light and dark chocolate browns, and then a mix of tans and yellows to match the Blaze's theme. Lights run along the dome's roof like white dashes on the road. Speakers hang in silence between the wooden-beamed lanes. Two long, industrial heater vents plush on the ceiling above both bleacher sections, spanning the length of the rink. And smack dab in the middle hangs the four-sided scoreboard.

"Hey, look," Barrett says. "It's our flag."

I trail his eyes to the city banners that decorate the towering wood wall. "Kielstad."

"And Prior Lake," he says. "That's ours." Prior Lake, the colors of navy blue and gold. And my Kielstad Knights, maroon, black, and white.

I stroll under the banners in a tight squeeze as the boards tempt to kiss the end wall. Through the glass, the zamboni rolls onto the ice and resurfaces the dirty sheet. It's suspicious of us to be sneaking around the glass in an uneventful rink, but hopefully the staff doesn't peel an eye on us. It'd make for an easier hunt.

A gate is locked up in chains to the side, allowing us to enter the far bleachers. The compass points forward. We step on the stairs and rise beside the mute yellow bleachers. Four rows of seating passed and we're at the top platform, surrounded by another lit trophy case, glowing in the dim corner of the arena. Trash and recycling bins organize themselves down the long platform. Me and Barrett follow the bins down the hall, searching for any of the hidden letters. The only words I see paint on the overhead heater-vents. Across the ice, the long, brown heater-vent has the words HOME and GARY R. HARKER RINK on it. The team benches also have the home and away signs, including a special whiteboard for the coaches to markup their anger and choices. It's tough trying to find a letter made from a wooden wall where it can easily camouflage itself in this rink. So much wood.

I check the compass again. It points through me. "Barrett," says I. I spin to him. "It's pointing back the way we came."

Barrett allows me to pass him. We return to the corner trophy case. And while the plastic players stare at me from within the trophy case, the compass points inside their home. Their secured home that is.

"Do you have a paperclip on you?" says I.

"No," Barrett says. "Let me check the recycling bin."

Barrett peeks inside of the blue bin. While the zamboni just made its turn around the near corner, I keep my attention on it. If the driver notices our suspicious scavenging, we're gonna end up being yelled at.

"Yes," Barrett says.

"Did ya find one?" says I.

"Not a paperclip," he says. "I found a hairpin on the floor though." He grabs it and drops it in my hand.

I hate hairpins. They litter everywhere, girls, or at least the majority of the users are girls. Some males do too, one's with extreme cabbage and mops, but most of those guys are on the ice playing the game.

Pulling the hairpin apart, I tickle the lock till a click unlocks the door. "Got it," says I.

"When in the icehouse did you learn to do that?" Barrett says.

I hand the puck compass to him. "Ash taught me tricks."

While the zamboni slows down at the far end of the ice, we squat down to the floor, pretending to be amazed at the vintage trophies. But while we're on the floor, we pick the case with our eyes, scanning for a wooden letter hiding inside.

"There's a lot to go through," Barrett says. "I mean like, it can be on top of the case too. Heck do we know."

"Maybe the compass can help again," says I. "Try it."

Barrett reaches his hand inside the case with the puck. The zamboni whips around again by us. My body blocks the view of Barrett's hand while the driver looks up. An older man he is, but he probably enjoys driving the zamboni.

When he drives the other way, I stand and amuse the compass. The stick whirls into a spin. It's flaring out of control.

"Don't move," says I. "It's here."

Barrett's hand floats inside of the case. The puck isn't above nor under a shelf. It can't be inside of a trophy if this compass is truly accurate. The light makes me squint as I check the roof of the trophy case. Nothing but a flat, wooden top. Nothing appears to be on the bottom either. I take my hand and feel around the trophies at the bottom, nothing but dust. My hand crawls to the wooden support beam for the case. The edges and crevices are smooth, but then something stabs my finger. It has to be it. I gently peel it from the beam, and with the twist of my palm lays the old, carved H.

"It was here," Barrett says. "It was actually here."

"I can't believe it," says I. "Feels like I'm holding history."

"That's cause you are," he says.

"And just to think a piece of The Barn was here the entire time, even when I had games here," says I.

Barrett's hand slows its vibration down from the compass' spinning. It redirects them. "Got our new location ready," he says.

"Awesome," says I. "Let's get out of here before someone spots us." I close the case to the display when the coast is clear to do so. The zamboni mops its last lane, coming forth to us. Before me and Barrett could even place a foot down on the concrete stairs, the gate unshackled itself. It slides shut with the chain swinging like a vine, wrapping itself on the gate and locking us up. Our feet scurry down to the steps. We crash into the gate, but it won't budge open.

The zamboni driver rolls by and stops behind the glass. He's not happy. "What the hell are you guys doing?" the old man says.

The zamboni explodes into a fireball. The old man's thrown from his seat. He smacks into the glass and lands on the ice, barrel-rolling the flames off. He seems to be okay, but his adrenaline's keeping the pain in the shadows for now. And like the gate's lock, me and Barrett can't unshackle words.

A rumbling and crumbling awaken inside the arena. It echoes across the ice like out on a frozen pond or an outdoor rink. The heater-vents swing in small beats, rocking back and forth like a crib. The lights strobe and fizz for the ghosts hopping on the ice for their game, electrifying the rink.

"I'm not liking this one bit," Barrett says.

"Me neither," says I. "Let's go around the other way."

A light bursts into a flamethrower. It shoots out napalm fire from the high-domed ceiling and licks the ice. The next light blows out, and then the next, and the next. They sync with one another, bursting down the length of the arena.

"Go, go, go!" says I. My hands push Barrett up the steps.

"There!" Barrett says. He points. "The fire alarm."

And beside the fire alarm, he's missing the treasure next to it. "And an emergency exit."

BOOM! The heater-vents blow smoke into the room, contaminating the air with its filthy pollution. We sprint to the emergency exit. While I crash through the door, the alarm rages from its handle, and Barrett pulls the fire alarm. The sprinklers ignite, but it's not water that sprays out. It's gasoline.

"Barrett," says I. "Let's go."

Barrett hops outside with me. The doors seal shut, locking the flames inside its oven.

"Well," Barrett says. "They're not wrong when they say the 'Burnsville Blaze.'"

When the words came out of his mouth, it sounded like a natural joke, but it makes me think about it more. "Do you have the hockey puck?"

"Yeah," he says.

"Let's get out of here," says I.

We trudge through the flakey snow and to the arena's parking lot. Firetrucks speed to the front entrance. We sneak to my SUV and head inside. An ambulance squeals its lights past us.

"We can't do this alone," says I.

"You think we caused that?" Barrett says.

"I know we did," says I. "I don't know if it was the puck that triggered it or what, but it had to have been us."

"At least we got what we came for," Barrett says. He holds up the letter H. "Wait, are you thinking of asking guys to join us?"

I nod.

"Who?" he asks.

DEPARTURE

Max and Miles undress in the shady locker room. Velcro unstraps all around. Sweat and snow soak the rubber mats that layer over the concrete floor. The brothers finished practice with their Junior hockey team, the Mankato Moose. While the two boys suffered under the dictation of their father, they turned out to be quite talented. They fought through Camp Kelmo, and nothing's going to stop them now.

While the sweat shop empties, Max and Miles plunk their remaining gear into their bags. Miles slithers out his cross necklace from the inside of his shoe. He clips the necklace on and stuffs his shoes onto his feet. Max waits patiently as his brother lags behind.

"Hold on," Miles says. "I'm coming." He throws the bag's strap over his shoulder and follows Max out the locker room door.

The frosting that tops the rink's boards are purple. The clean glass protects the empire of ice. Most of the rink is white, but on the back wall, presenting a line of windows, long enough to hold passengers on a private jet, has siding made of crisp-clean wood. It used to be where the home fans had to walk to if they wanted to cross to the other side of the rink. But now, it's a weight room, and it's on the second floor. People have to enter the arena, which is also on the second floor, then they have to walk past the small away-bleachers to the wooden back wall, enter through a door just to find stairs that loop to the first floor, skip past the concession stand which sells its goodies under the weight room, and then exit with the far door to walk up more steps where the bleachers await. Quite a hike for an indoor ice rink. Maybe the arena should build a bridge to connect the sides near the front wall. That would be lit.

Max and Miles push through the doors to leave the rink. The darkness dissolves them into the mini arcade and vending area, hiding in its tucked-away room. Smaller steps bring the boys to the bright front entrance. Mankato's All-Season Arena has two rinks. Their team got the high school's arena while the Bantam teams competed in the dinkier one. And there aren't too many arenas in Minnesota where the fans have to climb a flight of stairs just to enter the ice rink itself.

The twin brothers blast into the cold. They wander through the blocks of cars, shuffling through the street of frozen, crushed snow. The texture of the road isn't tar anymore but a flat surface of synthetic ice. When they stuff their bags in the trunk, Miles' phone vibrates in his pocket.

"Hello?" Miles says in the phone.

"Miles," says I. "It's Liam."

"Oh my God," Miles says. "Hey, Liam!" Max's eyebrows jolt up. "How are doing?"

"Well, we were doing good until we almost burned alive."

"What? Again?" Miles says. "The Barn's awake?"

"Not exactly," says I. "We found out how we can heal The Barn, but it turns out to me more dangerous than we thought."

"Wait," Miles says. "Who's we?"

"Me and Barrett," says I.

"That's right," he says. "I forgot you two live together now."

"Yeah," says I. "Miles, we need your guys' help. Do you and Max think you could ride with us up North?"

"Um," he says. Max shrugs his shoulders. "I doubt our father would accept."

"C'mon," says I. "We can't do this alone. And you guys are nineteen, right? You're adults now." At least were adults to the government. I never have the mindset of adulthood. I'll always be a child, no matter my age. It keeps me happy and motivated.

"I guess," Miles says. "We'll figure something out." Max nods in brotherly love. "Where should we meet?"

"Meet us in Burnsville at Homerun," says I. "You guys should be able to keep your car in the lot over the night or two."

"What are you doing there?" he asks.

"Lunch," says I.

"Pizza?" he says.

"You know me too well," says I.

"Alright," he says. "I'll let ya know when we're on our way."

"See ya," says I.

Miles slides his phone away. "Gonna have to sneak out of the house with our things," he says.

"We can make it happen," Max says.

"But how will we tell him we left?" Miles asks.

"Leave a letter behind," Max says.

"Saying what?" Miles says. "That we ditched him to go up North with some friends? He'll never forgive us."

"Miles," Max says. "It doesn't matter what he feels. He doesn't control our life anymore." Miles' face droops down in concern. "Look. We lived in a life full of no betrayal, and I understand that scares you, but I've been waiting for this day forever. Why don't ya say we live a little?"

Miles questions it, but Max pats him on the shoulder, pushing him to hop in the car and drive to the house. When they arrive, they storm to their shared room and pack away. Clothes, toothbrushes, treats, and waters.

Max writes a letter and leaves it on their bedroom's desk.

HOMERUN

The ambience of children's voices fills the building. Invisible
fumes rise into my nose from the fresh mozzarella pizza. Barrett
sits beside me on the plastic purple bench. I'm pretty sure this
place is based around baseball, hence the name, Homerun.
Baseball bats ting in the cages as kids whip away with them.
While Barrett's teeth clench in the thick cheese, I'm drawn to the
mini golf course. It's a pleasant area to eat. I watch the kids have
fun on the course, just like me when I was younger. This is one of
the nicer hangout spots near Kielstad. The tropical vibe this place
brings with fake palm trees, running streams, and pirate ships
makes for wonderful warmth.

Technically, we're not supposed to be here. At least we
bought food from the concessions, but you're supposed to have
wrist bands. Camouflaging within the groups of parents helps us
hide. Most of the kids running around are enough for the workers
to deal with.

Skeletons from the golf course's pirate ship dangle from the sails, and they stare right at us. I nudge my shoulder in front of it. Ha, now it can't see me. Well, I guess it still can, but it's great to have my back turned towards death.

"This pizza is da bomb, Liam," Barrett says.

"Not as good as Carbone's though," says I.

"It's cutting it close," he says.

"What do you like about it?" says I.

"The cheese," he says. "It's so gooey."

"Salty for sure," says I.

"Welcome to the tropics, where salt is in the air," he says. He's not wrong about the cheese. Mine keeps stretching from my mouth. I force my teeth into knives, breaking the stretch from my sauce-loaded lips. "Did your mom get us a hotel?"

"Yeah," says I. "An old place I've been to before. It's in Duluth, right on the waterfront."

"That's sick," Barrett says. "So, it's probably a fancy hotel?"

"Guess you could say that," says I. "The front entrance will blow you away."

Max and Miles arrive. They enter and plop a seat with us.

"God, those roads were rough," Miles says.

"Black ice?" says I.

"Yes," Miles says.

"And the roads have been hit with a few dozen asteroids," Max says.

"Yeah, those potholes could use some fat on them," says I. "You guys hungry?"

"I'm not," Miles says. "I should eat anyways though."

"Go ahead," say I. "You two can finish it off." They grab their slices off the cardboard.

"Where are we traveling to?" Miles says.

"We're not sure," Barrett says.

"We found this compass," says I. My hand slides the puck on the table. "The owner of The Barn had a son. He led us to it."

"What does it do?" Miles says.

"It leads the way," says I.

"To what?" Max asks.

"Puzzle pieces," says I. "We need to collect them."

"They're engravings from The Barn," Barrett says.

"Mr. Muckens was the son of the owner," says I. "He said his father engraved four letters from that outdoor shed. H-E-double hockey sticks."

"Hell," Miles says. "Sure, it's a coincidence, but how does that turn The Barn to life?"

"It doesn't," says I. "The Barn has always had a life of its own, but it's been hurt."

"Vandalized," Barrett says.

"Still don't get how a rink killed our friends," Max says.

"I know it's hard to believe," says I. "You weren't there when it was awake."

"You'll see what we mean," Barrett says, taking over the conversation. "These letters hide in hockey rinks. We're not certain why his father hid them at the rinks, but these traps we encounter will make you believe."

"We almost burned to death inside of Burnsville's rink," says I. "And I don't think the Muckens invented it. Every place has a life of its own, and it'll do anything in its power to protect itself."

"I guess stealing property ticked it off," Barrett says.

"The letter didn't belong to it though," says I. "It was The Barn's belonging."

"Places can be a bitch too," Barrett says.

"Wait, you found a letter?" Max says.

I slide the H on the table. "We got three more to go." Max and Miles stuff down their last bites of the pizza's doughy crust. Grease and flour stick to my hand. I wipe my fingers off with a napkin, not that it does much help with the grease. I grab the compass and H, sliding them in my pocket, then search for a sink to wash my hands in. The guys stay back while I wander around the party palace.

Passing the front desk of prizes, a dark room explodes in neon lights and pixels. Powerups, pews, slaps, throws, rolls, bleeps, and bits create chaos for a child's casino. I'm sucked into the aisles of games, watching kids race each other with fake foot pedals and steering wheels, rolling skee-balls on their track, hunting pixelated animals in the woods, and ripping down a lever to a spinning wheel of luck.

A machine speaks into my ears. "Hello, racer." Jolting around, a snowmobiling game awaits for my three tokens. "Insert three tokens for an adventure of a lifetime." I shake my head and turn around. "Where are you going, Liam?" No way. I spin back to the machine. Gradually, I place myself on the seat of the machine, reclining my back on the plastic. Foot pedals and a steering wheel patiently rest for a touch.

A boy beside me loses in a formula race. "Hey, kid," says I. "Can you spare three tokens for me?"

"Screw off, buckaroo," he says.

"Excuse me?" says I.

"You heard me," he says.

"What if I paid you?" says I.

"I don't want money," he says.

"What do you want then?" says I.

"Your tickets," he says.

"I'll tell you what," says I, ready to bargain with a twelve-year-old. "If you give me three tokens, I'll win first place for ya."

"And if you don't, you have to pay me in tickets and cash."

"Fine. Deal." What did I just get myself into?

He hands me three gold coins. I slide them into the coin slot. The machine whirls up in snow, wiping away the home screen to a map selection. "Choose a track," the machine says.

"Moscow," the boy says. He shakes my shoulders, begging for that track. At least it's an easy level.

"Moscow it is," says I.

I select Moscow. The screen changes to sled options. Red's always the fastest. Red it is. Eventually, the race turns on. The machine counts down from three. Once the horn flares, we're off to the race. I floor the acceleration pedal down, sledding in the middle of the other racers.

We grind through snow inside of a palace, lightened with

hanging chandeliers of gold. I speed past three of the sleds out of twelve, ditching them behind my dirt, or snow for that matter. Whooshing past all the lights, I ramp up onto escalators, leading to the outdoor portion of track. The track banks side to side with the turns inside of Moscow's Russian architecture, most buildings made from stone and concrete. The Russian flag hangs upon the light posts that litter the edges of the track. A snowbank splits the track into two. Other racers push me to the bottom portion of the track. I'm sliding into a snow-bounded subway tunnel with curved, white arches and golden etchings in the walls. Suddenly, the tunnel leads to an uphill where I find myself leaping in the air, hovering over other riders returning from the upper portion of the split. We merge together, me leading in sixth place. A sharp turn to the right brings me to a literal jump. My snowmobile soars into the air while I pull off a trick, letting my legs fly off the ride and through the falling snow. I slam into the ground, trying to regain my control back. A train's horn blares in front of my ride. I swerve out of its way. The snowmobile behind me crashes into its front. I'm in fourth place, and the finish line is coming up soon. Glass shatters as I smack into a tunnel's entryway. The four of us in the lead boost onto a bridge's walkway. In fury, I floor the pedal as far down as I can, speeding past all the spherical lights in the walkway. I zoom past two of the players, coming in second place. A gigantic snow jump lifts us into a parking ramp. I dodge through the support beams and nick my head against the low concrete ceilings. Another jump propels me into a construction site. The finish line is ahead, and the first-place rider is right in front of me.

My sled hovers in the air as I soar like a bird in the clouds. I just leaped out of the skyscraper's construction site. And while I float in the air, I tilt my body back, ready to land this puppy. BLAM. My machine rattles as it hits the ground. I floor the pedal one last time, zipping by first place who lost landing control. I rip through the ribbon, winning first place.

"Great job, Liam," the machine says.

The creeps chill back to my bones. I check to see where the kid went, but he's not in sight. "How do you know my name?" says I. "How can you speak?"

"You're right when you say we all have a life of our own."

"Wait," says I. "You can talk to me?"

"Why of course! We all have a voice of our own."

"What do you want with me?" says I.

"It's not what I want from you, it's what I want to say to you. I overhead your conversation with your friend."

"How do you know my name?" I ask.

"When you talked with your friend, of course." A brief moment fades back when Barrett said, 'This pizza is da bomb, Liam.' Kinda creepy, but I guess I got more things to worry about.

"What did you want to tell me?" says I.

"I can see your emotions. I can feel your fear. It's like you tremble in my stomach of arcade machines and mini golf."

"I'm not scared, just nervous for my friends," says I.

"And that's fear hiding itself. You must not let fear take control of your anxiety. You must fight through it."

"But what if something happens to them?" says I. "Everyone

around me has been getting hurt. Finn, Charlie, Orson, Shawn—"

"Your friends are here for you, Liam. They don't have to be here if they don't want to, but they do. They're here to help you." My self-doubt sneaks back into my stomach. "I can hear them talking about you right now."

"What are they saying?" I ask.

"The two guys are saying they love you and your friend. They're always going to be there for you, no matter what the cost." I lie back in the plastic chair again, flushing out the tears. I've never had any siblings, but I have brothers now. They fill the holes in my heart.

A hand rips the tickets out from the machine. I discover the boy's laugh sinking into my mouth. Something's not right about this kid. He wants me to see something. And I see it. The letter H has slipped out from my sweats. It's contained in his hand.

"Give it back," says I. "Now."

He giggles. He sprints away from me. I launch off from my chair and sprint through the dancing lights of the arcade. The kid runs in the open lobby and into a play palace. When I make it inside the palace, tunnels and tubes and bridges and slides create one heck of an amusement park. This is a literal maze of torture.

The boy crawls up the matted stairs and into the netted maze. I crawl up the tubular rubber steps and end up on the second floor. A girl runs out from the hanging boxing bags. A thud draws me to the boy as he crawls into a tunnel. I run on over and crawl inside the small tube. At the end of the tunnel, the boy runs across a bridge and into the swinging boxing bags. I push a few small aliens out of my way, checking through the boxing bags. The boy waits for his turn on the slide as I have him cornered.

"Give me that," says I. He shakes his head. I pull out my wallet and fan out a twenty-dollar bill. "If you give me it back, you can buy more tokens with this." He rips the bill out from my hand. He throws the H letter down the slide. I shove the kids out of my way and dart down the slide. I slip to the bottom and receive the letter back.

A smile grows on my face. I hold the letter H in the air and cheer in victory. I'm the king of the castle now. That is until security meets me with crossed arms. One of the aliens I pushed on the course runs by in tears.

"Whoopsies," says I.

BEARS

The outskirts of Edina and Minnetonka make me wanna puke. This is why I hate the cities. There are mansions and castles and palaces showing off their owners with fortune under their platinum belts. No wonder why these two cities raised amazing professional hockey players. If you have money, you have easier opportunities, or at least simpler access to things I wouldn't even have the chance to think about. Expensive hockey camps and gear and coaches, they can pay for it all in cash. And other than my jealousy, Edina's the main problem, thinking they own every rink they go into. The Edina Eagles have too many wins under their wings, and it's all thanks to their spoiled lives. Part of me knows there are still human beings with feelings in that city, but a true hero would lend me some leftover money.

A vibration wakes in Barrett's hand. As I drive on the two-laned freeway, crossing over a bridge, the hockey stick points to the right, stabbing its way through the door.

"Turn off here," says Barrett. I steer the vehicle onto the ramp, which turns sharper than me on the ice; if I turned that sharp, I'd be sliding into a new dimension, or at least I should know to slow down before making a super sharp turnoff.

"Hopkins?" Miles says.

"Not Hopkin's school," says I. "Blake."

"The Blake Bears," Max says. "I remember this arena!"

"Same here," says I. "How could you not? It's got the curved wooden roof, and the old school locker rooms."

"It's been a while for me," Barrett says.

"Did we play here, Max?" Miles asks.

"Yes," Max says. "This is the one where we stood on the bleachers, and when we watched coach draw stuff up on the bench, there was the illusion that the roof was collapsing on top of us, with the curvature and all."

"Guess we'll find out," Miles says. "I have to see it again."

The stoplight crosses me over city tracks. I pull into the arena's parking lot, sitting beneath the football stadium and the school on the neighboring hill. The Hopkins bland water tower is skyscraping behind the rink's fuming pipes of steam, releasing into the cold air. This hockey rink has always been an oddity. The entrance sits on the left, and the arena's roof is shaped like a crescent moon sticking out from the frozen cement. Bantam's was the last time I played here. It was always a close game versus the Bears.

We exit my car and head to the side doors in a bundled bunch. Déjà vu. A double set of french doors lead us into the

72

arena, an updated entrance. It's so clean, fresh, and stenches of fresh paint. The high school player's locker room is on my immediate right, waiting for the animals to leave their cave. That's what the players call their locker room. The Bear Cave. I miss the old craftsman work they had on the wall which resembled the cave's exterior. But it appears it's gone.

Wooden trophy cases hold the old tin awards as we move into the main facility. The ice sheet hasn't changed. The roof still domes over the hockey game. It's quiet though. No hockey is scheduled during the day, I guess. That'll make this search much easier. If our assumption is correct, the letter E hides in here.

I stumble my way onto the bleachers, the newly updated seating area. All the old, wood benches people sat on are gone, replaced with fancy cement ones. I can no longer see the pipes that hung behind the bleachers, right over the tops of the old locker rooms. There's even a fricken walkway over the hall we'd use to get to the crummy locker rooms. Wow. This place has jumped into the future.

Beneath the new walkway is the corridor to the sparkling locker rooms. The ceiling is tin, and the modern lights trail our eyes to the end wooden wall. Peeking inside of the locker rooms, I could sense how much space these locker rooms grew.

"Sad to see the kids won't know what dingey locker rooms were like anymore," Barrett says.

"Really?" Max says. "It's about time they made more space."

"I remember this rink now," Miles says. "The old locker rooms were tight tunnels. You could barely even see each other

73

with how dark the lighting was."

"I'm with Barrett on this one," says I. "I'm going to miss the traditional dusty, muggy rooms, whether the outlets near the fricken ceiling worked or not."

The lights die out. Inside the locker room is the vastness of darkness. Light fades in from the daylight at the other end of the corridor near the doors, but other than that, it's pitch-black inside. The rink's manager pops at the end of the hall, casting his way to the doors with a flashlight. He's marching with anger, almost as if it has happened before.

I pull out my phone for a modern flashlight as Miles copies. "Let's go," says I. "This is our chance." While I move down the hall in a stealthy walk, the boys tiptoeing behind me, my breath frosts up in front of my lips. Hockey rinks are cold, but this one just blew in an ice storm.

"Anyone else get the chills?" Miles says.

"Yeah," Barrett says. "It's fricken freezing. Liam, where's the compass point to?"

"Let me see," says I. I scavenge my pocket, sliding out the hockey puck. I lift my head to the front entrance. "Straight."

No one's in sight. The compass points to the high school's locker room. I sneak the guys past the set of doors and into the dark, mini corridor. The doors to the boy's and girl's locker rooms are on the left. But at the end of the hall, the darkness doesn't just end. A tunnel of wind tempts to swift our bodies into the depths of the hallway. The boys freeze in their feet behind me as I move forward.

"Liam?" Barrett says.

My eyes widen at the picture that presents itself. I turn the flashlight off on my phone. "Miles," says I. "Turn your light off." Miles shuts it down.

"What do you see, Liam?" Barrett says.

"Eyes," says I. "Bat eyes."

Hundreds of eyes glow around the lighted stalagmites and stalactites of ancient rock. Puddles of water reflect the cathedral of mother nature's painting.

"A cave?" Miles says.

"Not just any cave," says I. "A bear cave."

"Pretty big cave for a bear," Max says.

"I'm not so sure we should be worried about the size of the cave, Max," says I.

A bat flutters its wings to a new hanging spot. Glowing webs of saliva hang above us as we shimmy inside the cold cave. On the webs aren't spiders but glowing worms. They illuminate the cave's ceiling into a Milkyway Galaxy of stars.

"What are those?" Barrett asks.

"Glowworms," Max says. My eyes glow blue in their light. "They glow from their feeding, catching prey in their webs."

"It's like an oil rain lamp," says I.

"A raining what?" Miles says.

"An oil rain lamp," says I. "Oil drips down fishing string in the shape of a rounded gazebo. My grandma had one."

"They made em in the seventies for décor," Max adds.

"Old people are strange," Miles says.

We reach a dark dead end. And resting upon a natural pedestal is the letter. E. "I found it," says I.

"Well, that was easy," Barrett says.

I sprint to the letter and grasp my hand around it. I lift it off the pedestal and show the guys. "We did it," says I. Two eyes open behind the pedestal. It huffs and puffs in the cave's dead spot. "Guys. Move back slowly." The eyes float in the dark, moving around the pedestal. It's furry foot steps into the light. The bear's face pokes out from the dark, inching closer and closer.

"I don't like this one bit," Miles says.

"Just don't run," Max says. "Take it easy."

The cave rumbles into a shake. Pebbles from the rock ceiling bounce off of my head. The sword of a stalactite crackles off the ceiling and explodes in front of me. "Run!" says I. Its fall splits us from the bear, but it finds its way around and chases us. Bats soar past our heads, almost knocking us to our knees. Checking behind me, the bear dodges falling knives of rock, catching up to the dust we kick behind. "Hurry!" Stalactites collapse in front of our clear path to the arena.

Miles points off to the side. "Over here!" He sprints us over to a reflective mirror of water.

"How deep is that?" Max asks.

The bear growls its teeth behind me. "No time for questions."

Miles leaps into the water. "Miles!" Max yells. Miles pops above the water and swims to the exit. "I'm not swimming in that."

"Oh, yes you are," Barrett says. Barrett shoves Max into the water. Me and Barrett jump into the glacier-cold water. We paddle our way to the edge as the bear steps into our rippling waves. It dives deep into the pond. "Let's go!" Barrett reaches the edge while Miles tries and pulls him out. Max reaches his arms out for me. I grab hold of them. I push off the edge of rock with my shoes, shoving my weight out from the water. As we pant on the cave's floor, bubbles burst on top of the pond. Then, they stop.

"Let's get out of here," says I.

We exit the cave and revisit the front entrance. The lights turn back on, blinding us with no preparation. Bats cloud up the rink, twisting in their manmade tornado.

We got what we came for. It's time to dash out.

Back in the car, we recoup ourselves.

"You guys were right," Miles says. "These traps are killers."

"Yeah," Max says. "Not cool."

"Actually, that was pretty cool," Miles says.

"We almost turned into a bear's meal," he says.

"These places really do have a life of their own," Miles says.

"Yes," says I. "That's why we need to heal The Barn."

"Where to next, Liam?" Barrett asks.

"Let's see where the puck takes us, hopefully North. That's where our hotel is. Duluth." The hockey stick points up, and as I hop onto the freeway, it takes us North on 35, out of the metro.

OVERNIGHTER

Ducking under a bridge of a coal-liner's tracks, Duluth presents its picturesque view from the hills. The Blatnik and Aerial Lift Bridge anchor their concrete supports into the slushy waters of Lake Superior. Most of the port shackles in hexagonal shapes of ice, but the icebreakers will shatter them to glass when they float through. The boys wake up from the dull drive of bare trees and flat snowfields. Altitude made notice in our ears, clogging them with invisible tissue paper. But maybe it was the excitement of the hill that woke them up. Barrett doesn't show any signs of fear from the hill's height, the darkness may lessen the fear. My anxiety will turn on if I have to drive on the icy roads in the city that ramp you up to space.

While I'm driving, a billboard advertises a game of laser tag at Journeyland. That's an activity I'll pass on. Piles of ore from the iron range chill in the cold near the train's end of tracks. We find the Amsoil Arena where the collegiate Bulldogs play. My junior year of high school, we watched a game from the upper stands. The memory lingers in the back of my mind in a forgotten chest.

Factories and shops and bridges clutter in as we reach the heart of the city. Ships ported in the harbor act as monsters; if they had teeth in the front, they could munch down an entire block of buildings. Duluth sits where the river meets Lake Superior, and the lake mimics the horizon line of an ocean.

I turn onto Lake Avenue as the road renames itself to Canal Park Drive. The city turns itself into a European village with cobblestone sidewalks and vintage lampposts. Yellow lines on the road lead the eye to the sculpture of the Aerial Lift Bridge, hovering over the snow-bounded buildings.

Our hotel is on the left, right on the shore of Lake Superior. Mom reserved a room at the hotel I stayed at on that hockey trip junior year. That year was a quick trip, but it was very much a memorable one. We played in the Amsoil rink and the ancient Heritage Center. Ash and I roomed together with Thomas and Chester. We stayed in our bunch while the first liners did their own thing.

Parking in the packed lot, we carry our suitcases inside. Inside the entrance, a balcony from the second floor overlooks onto a courtyard of cozy furniture. Receptionists hide behind the desks in the middle of the hotel. A line of windows creates a canvas of the North Shore where an old, small concrete structure drowns in the ice. That's the historic Mausoleum. It's a sinister thing that was supposed to house the rotting corpses of humans above ground, but it now just gets slammed with wild waters from

Lake Superior.

We check in with the front desk, then they hand Barrett and I two cards to the hotel room. Carrying our luggage again, we march up the steps to the second floor and roll along to our room. Scanning my card over the keypad, the door clicks open. I push it open to our room that overlooks frozen Lake Superior. Me and Barrett lay our stuff on the bed near the window while Max and Miles set theirs by the other one.

"Barrett," says I. "Keep your card. That'll be ours." I hand mine to Max. "You guys can have this one."

"Sick," Max says.

"Wait," Miles says. "I think I should have it."

"No," Max says. "You're more capable of losing it than me."

"Nah uh," he says. "You're more capable of breaking it."

"Not true," Max complains.

"Liam?" they say in sync.

"How bout this?" says I. "You two will switch off every hour, and we'll see who takes better care of it."

"Fine," Miles says. "You can have the first hour."

Barrett tosses clothes out from his suitcase.

"Barrett?" says I.

He spins around with trunks balled up in his hands. His cheeks puff up with a jovial smile. "Beat ya to the hot tub." Barrett runs into the bathroom and locks the door shut, beating Max to it.

"Aren't there changing rooms in the pool room anyway?" says I. Max and Miles send each other the look, then they transmit their idea directly to me. We all rip our trunks from our bags and crash out the room's door.

Barrett unlocks the door and notices the clutter of clean clothes all over the beds. He takes the key card and leaves the room with his loss. Barrett walks down the steps, passes the courtyard of furniture, and follows the signs to the pool. When he slides into the humid room, he places his things down near our stuff on the table and cannon balls in the hot tub, cascading waves to chloroform us. We're soaked in the relaxing tub of chlorinated water. As our laughing settles, so do the waves. The jets fume streams of fizz on our backs, massaging us in comfort.

"Why can't we do this every day?" Miles says. His cross necklace tickles the water.

"Right?" Barrett says.

"Not the best for your body the night before a game though," Max says. "It'll relax your muscles too much. You'll be skating off your heavy blubber rather than playing the game."

"I found that out the hard way," says I. "Too much swimming. I've never enjoyed swimming anyways. My legs pull me under the surface every time."

"Need stronger abs," Barrett says. I backhand him in the stomach. He knows I was joking, but it probably still hurt a little. I'm the strongest one here, even if you can't see my armor. "That kinda hurt."

"Too strong for ya?" says I.

"Nah," he says. "Wanna see real strength?" Barrett climbs out from the pot of boiling water and leaps into the pool. He splashes into the cool water, disturbing its peace. His head pokes out from the sizzling bubbles. "Your turn."

"I hate cold water," says I.

"C'mon," he says. "Show me your brave enough."

"Fine," says I. "This'll prove nothing." I hop out of the hot tub and shuffle my way over to the edge of the pool. Sorta reminds me of the dreams I got where I was in the pool, but the edge was too high for me to reach. I could see the surface of beach chairs that people relaxed upon, but I was trapped in the pool's pit.

With no second thought, I take lift off. My feet slam into the water, sending a shockwave through my body. My hair soaks into a mop as my feet land at the bottom. I push back above water, hating myself for doing this, but it isn't too bad. I'm already used to the difference.

"That wasn't too bad," says I.

"I was just kidding," Barrett says. "I just wanted to torture you into jumping in with me."

"Hey," says I. "I was still brave."

"Wanna see bravery?" Miles says. He sprints and leaps at us. Water cascades over us in an intense downpour. We meet eyes with each other above the waves, hacking up the swallowed chemicals. "Join us, Max."

Max shakes his head. "I'm good."

Me, Barrett, and Miles tiptoe out of the pool, leaving the water undisturbed of trickles. We sneak behind him. Miles grabs him under the armpits and pulls him out. Barrett and I grab onto his feet. We bring him to the side of the pool. Counting down from three, Max flies into the cool water. We jump in the wild waters again, joining him in the fun.

After a splendid hour in the springs of hot and cold, I change into different clothes and play knee hockey in the hallway outside our room. I'm playing goalie for me and Barrett, and Max plays goalie for him and Miles. With the foam ball, Miles whips a shot with his stick. The ball bounces off of my arm, then deflects off the wall to my stick. Barrett crawls his knees to the side, opening for a pass, but Miles blocks him off. Instead, I rip a shot off the opposite wall. The ball ricochets under Max's foot. It hits his ankle and rolls into the net.

I throw my hands in the air for a classic celly, but since I score all the time, I should rub the dust off from my shoulders instead. Duh.

"Lucky goal," Miles says.

"More like slick skills," says I.

"Oh, c'mon. You didn't even aim for the net."

"I did too. You're just jealous."

"Whatever," he says. His pout is quite comical.

My throat dries in dehydration. "Hold on, guys. Imma grab some fruit punch quick."

"Bring me a bottle," Max says.

I close the door behind me softer than a stuffed animal chewing on cotton candy. The mini fridge sits under the television in its cubby space. I prop it open and grab two bottles of fruit punch. A vibration of a phone steals my attention. I close the fridge, set the drinks down, and pick my buzzing phone up.

"Hello?" says I, answering it with an assumption of another

stupid scammer. I probably shouldn't answer it, but who knows, maybe it's a hockey scout desperately calling out my name for me to join their team. It isn't though. It's a voice I don't want to here.

"Liam," Investigator says. "We have a serious problem. Seventeen squirts just got hospitalized from a phenomenon of melting ice and a strategic falling of a light pole at the outdoor Kielstad hockey rink, electrocuting them in a matter of seconds. I'm no scientist, but ice on a very cold day doesn't just melt on its own, and the timing of the light was just perfect."

"Oh my God," says I. "Are they alright?"

"No deaths have been reported yet, but the hospital has seventeen hockey players in shock right now. Some of the kids have cuts from the shattered bulbs, and a couple of them had their legs and arms crushed by that pole."

"Geezes," says I. "I don't know what to say."

"Well, you better find something."

"Wait. You think I did this?"

"Let me tell you what I think. I think you know something that would be of value to me. I don't think a nineteen-year-old boy would attempt to murder squirts at their nighttime practice. But a boy who runs away from town in the middle of all this draws me in. It's like peanut butter to a puppy."

"How can I explain this without you freaking out at me?"

"I know more about you than you could imagine," he says. "Why would Miss Moriz traumatize hockey players at a summer camp, specifically the ones who had graduated high school that year?"

"Cause of her son," says I. "Clayton."

"It had nothing to do with his accident," Investigator says. "She made Camp Kelmo because of you."

"Because of me?" says I.

"She was always trying to get to you," he explains. "Annie dreamt about The Barn. She was fascinated about the events that happened there your senior year. She studied you."

"Why me?" says I. "Why'd it have to be me?"

"You were the weakest. The most vulnerable."

"You're lying," says I. "How would you even know? She's dead. And you didn't know her beforehand."

"Actually, I did," he says. "It was until the time she ripped Clayton from my hands that I had forgotten her."

"You're not his father," says I. "I saw Clayton's father pick him up last summer at the rink."

"Marriage is a mirage," he says.

"That was Clayton's step-father?" says I.

"Unfortunately, yes," he says. "Annie had bi-polar issues in her heart, if she had one that is. I discussed appointing her to a rehabilitation center, but that's when she flipped at me. She took my son away and never returned."

"And now his stepfather is letting him live with him?"

"I can take my son back," he says, "but Clayton doesn't know me too well. Annie kept him locked out from my life."

"I know he's desperate to see his biological father for once," says I. "I wish I could see my father again." The Investigator is silent. Only a cool breeze gusts over his side of the phone. The door opens behind me.

"You coming back out?" Barrett asks.

I hold up my pointer finger to him. He exits. "Imma go here," says I. "Please let me know any updates on the kids." The Investigator stills in more silence. I cut the call.

THE DEAD

The heater hums in the blackness of the hotel room. Minnesota barely spots the moon in the wintertime. Usually, the cold tags along with overcast clouds. But the sky starches from the city lights, and with the curtains closed above the heater, no light pokes inside. I never thought about Barrett inside of a hotel room. I hope it doesn't traumatize him. His parents cut the AC vent open, poisoning themselves in suicide. At least I'm by the vent and not him. His back is turned away from me. Miles and Max snore soft on their bed. See, they both snore. I knew they both had to have the genes together as identical twins.

While I'm not too tired, I sure attempt to doze off after the drive. I can't seem to sleep with hold of the letters, and yet missing a couple more. Hopefully, it won't be too long till we dig them up from their hiding spots. Tomorrow, we'll follow the hockey puck again. Recently, it points to the northwest. As long as it doesn't break us through the Canada border, everything should work well.

I've never had a great sleep in a hotel before. The beds are always hot, the sheets mess up, blankets are thick with feathers, and the pillows flip hundreds of times in the night. Sleeping on the ground might be the easiest option here. I turn to my side, hoping the sweet spot improves my sleep. I close my eyes, forcing them to not open. The eyelids are stitched together, I'm not allowing them to open without my approval.

My feet soak in waves of water. The sheets stick to me in the humid heat. My head sways up and down upon the pillow. I'm dehydrated probably. Or more food may help. I sense a light headiness creeping inside of my energy tank. I'm running low on energy. Sleep deprived. And even with my argument I revved up about keeping my eyes shut, sleep is not an option for me. My body tells me to move.

I open my eyes. The water. It's surreal. My sheets, pillow, and my body transported somewhere bizarre, or so reality kicked me in another dimension. Old concrete walls hide the darkness from outside. And a moon in the cloudless sky adds light in the structure. The floor beneath me slants into the water, sinking into the unknown abyss. It's cold water too. My body wants out.

I toss the sheets off from me. I'm bathing in the cold water with my clothes on. Standing up from the floor, the water trickles off of my shirt. The ripples disturb the peaceful water from my motions. They continue to wave to the walls of the noticeable structure. I feel like I've seen this place before.

A dark shadow rises from the bottom of the slanted floor. It's slow and soothing to watch. Another shadow bends out from underneath the water. They're shaped like small, deformed globs. My hand attracts to it like honey to a bumblebee. Nothing stops my urge to reach out to the glob. My fingertips tip the cold water as the glob connects to them. Warmth. Nice, warm water.

I detach my hand from the water. Bam! Another hand slaps around my arm. It pulls me to the water as I fight its strength. My feet slip on the mossed-up floor beneath my sockless feet. My face heads to the water, right where I meet a smiling, rotting skeleton. It drags my head under the water, locking its soul onto mine. My chest begs for air as I choke on my own breath. Bubbles cough out from my mouth, rising to the surface that waves upon my neck.

My second wind blows in. I grab hold of the skeleton's hand upon my arm, ripping away its joints from it. The bones crack with crust and rust and muss as they crumble one by one. The skeleton screeches underwater. I release myself from the water and intake gallons of air above. To the side of the room, a hallway with windows opens up my opportunity to escape this rememberable place. And when I leave for the hall, rectangular cutouts in the concrete present a picturesque view to the outside. I can't see anything but the giant lake.

I'm on the mausoleum in Lake Superior. An above ground grave for the dead. But the city of Duluth isn't there. It's almost as if a mirror reflects the lake back to me, blocking out the city lights. It's tough to trudge through the mass of cold water on the slippery slope. The whole structure slants downwards. And to the right of my feet, the floor disappears. It eroded away, cracked from the

89

structure. One wrong step and I could be sinking into the bottom of the dark depths.

Bam! Many hands dart out from the side of the eroded floor, reaching for my ankles. I bounce back to the wall of windows, avoiding their ghostly grips. Screeches bubble out from the water, but a deadly scream amplifies behind me. The water splish-splashes. The arms and hands sink back into the lake. A calm splashing from a ghosts' pair of legs approaches closer and closer. I slosh backwards down the floor as the water rises. And the invisible force follows me, step by step. Behind me, I dare to look for an exit. But as I do, an open window presents itself for me.

Splish-splashes turn violent into water bombs. The invisible force sprints at me in the water. I book it down the hall as the mass stomps louder and louder. My hips force through the cold water as I make it to the window. Without hesitance, I take a leap of faith out from the window and dive into the water.

A light shine on my face. I open my eyes under the water. My feet hit the clean floor. I launch off the floor and rise my head out from the wavy surface. I'm in the hotel's pool. But the ledges of the pool, they're higher than they should be. Swimming over to them, I'm desperate to climb out, but my hands can't reach the top. And above me is Coach Kipp, looking down upon me. He laughs as I'm stuck in the water.

I yell for help, but nothing leaves my throat. From under the deep end of the bunked-in pool, a giant, rectangular, plastic filter blows away as the water drains into the huge hole. My body is pulled in the direction of it. The pool water whirls in a massive circle, spiraling down towards the drain. I'm waterboarded from the waves as my body is cascaded with the wild water. I swirl and swirl as the walls grow tall. "Liam?"

A hand taps on my shoulder. The daylight seeps through the curtains of the hotel room. The hands tap at my shoulder again. I shiver and hide under the sheets.

"Liam?" Barrett says.

After a few moments of nothing, I retract myself from the blankets. On the other side of the bed is Barrett. He stares at me.

"Barrett," says I. "Oh. I'm sorry. I just woke up from a nightmare."

"Really?" he asks. "You were startled there waking up."

"That was so weird," says I. "It's like I woke up with extreme tunnel vision. I didn't know if I was awake, I guess."

"Well, Max and Miles are ready for breakfast. I am too. We should probably get going here if we want to get those letters."

My mind forgot about the letters there. But waiting any longer kills time and children at The Barn. The mausoleum sure is haunted. Opening the curtains to the blinding daylight, there it lurks, in the frozen waters of Lake Superior, taunting me.

THE BUNKER

Down at the continental breakfast, I skip the chemically induced cinnamon rolls and instead pour waffle mix into the machine. It cooks my giant waffle in the matter of minutes. Mini maple syrup containers pile inside of a basket. I steal three and grab a seat by Barrett and the twins. My mouth devours the sweetness of the syrup and wafer bread. The sun peeks over the horizon behind the cold waters of Lake Superior. Clouds will eventually blow over for a typical overcast day in Minnesota.

After breakfast, we pack our things and leave the hotel with the sunrise. Throwing our luggage in my car, we head onto the freeway again, following the compass. From 35, I merge onto 2 for a long scenic route into the flats of forest and snowbound land. Most of the travel pulls us through podded forests, but once we pass Grand Rapids, the frozen lakes left from the remanence of a gigantic glacier covers the land. Two hours into the drive, I lag through Bemidji, dodging a state trooper in town, and watch the compass twist North. Another hour later, we're coasting into a small town. We're on the outskirts of the Canada border.

"No way," says I.

"What is it?" Barrett says.

"We're in Roseau." Sleeping Max awakens from his morning nap to the sound of my voice. "I played here my Bantam year. I remember that day. It was below zero, the guys bought Boa sticks from that cool hockey shop, and it was my first game ever to be kicked out of."

"What did you do?" Barrett asks.

"I may have accidently had too much adrenaline in my system and charged a guy by our bench. Then I slammed him from behind. He collapsed to the ground pretty hard, but he got up in fury just fine."

"You don't seem like a guy who'd get a major," Miles says. "No offense."

"None taken," says I. "Everyone said the same thing."

There it is. The compass points to the treasure of Roseau's Memorial Arena. Many NHL and Olympic players were born in this arena. History lives inside the pine that the farmer's logged up together. This place is ancient, over fifty years old like my rink. It has a deep soul.

Exiting the car, we approach the cold steps to the bunker's entrance, or so the ice arena is domed like an airplane's bunker. Inside, the front warming room is small. Wood panels cover the wall in a vertical formation, and office ceiling tiles enlighten the room. Pictures pop from the walls with awards, old teams, photographs of the NHL players who played here as a kid, and other neat knick knacks. Barrett and Miles are pulled into the vintage gold, but Max's attention is grabbed to the arena. On the ice, the boy's high school team practices.

"I hope a college picks me up," Max says. "I know I made juniors, but that can only get me so far." I'm out of words while I haven't tried out for any junior team. It makes me salty thinking about it. How did these guys figure out their route to success?

"Don't stress about it," says I. "Dude, at least you have an opportunity. No one ever told me about hockey after high school, no matter how hard I worked on myself." I can't not stress about hockey though. The stress is what drives me to do what I do, and maybe it's telling me something more with hockey. Maybe my career hasn't ended yet, I just can't envision the future.

"How am I supposed to compete with these guys?" he says. "My brother scores more goals than I do. We're not even on the same line."

"Don't let anything destroy your relationship with your brother," says I. "Colleges love seeing those stats, but some of them would rather hire a player who has speed, strength, and an extreme passion for the sport. If you'd sacrifice your life for hockey, then your mentality is there. You just have to break through that fear of failure. It's okay to fail."

"What are you going to do?" Max says.

"Huh?" says I.

"It's obvious your good at hockey," he says. "Why aren't you still playing?" I think over that for a second. Yes, no one has told me where I should go in life, but I'm still nineteen. I'm still young enough. "Can I tell you what I think? I think you have doubts, and those doubts are what's holding you back."

"Doubts?" says I. "Like what?"

"Possibly teammates from high school," he says. "Or your coaches. Maybe you focused too much on them and not enough on yourself."

He's right. As much as I hate to admit it. Why was I so caught up in their game and not my own? Of course, I wanted to be the goal scorer and legend of Kielstad, but my skills weren't fully developed. My thoughts were too busy scrambling around about the coaches playing the other lines more. But still, they weren't any better than I was. So, why did coach still overload them on the ice and not me? Was I emotionally the weakest, the easiest player to be cheated upon?

In a hurry to hide my tears, I storm out of the room and follow the rubber padding to the nearest stairs.

"Liam?" Max says. Barrett and Miles notice me leaving the room. Max looks back at them, then he watches me enter the ice arena from above. The rink is cold, but the coach's whistle is warmly inviting. Roseau is home of the Rams. The guys skate in a full-ice drill, flowing puck passes from one line to the next. The pucks remind me of my reasoning for being here.

I check the puck compass in my hand. It points at one o'clock. That's where the zamboni room is, on the other side of the bunker. There's no easy way to get around these old wooden bleachers, and I don't want to look like an oddball child in front of these guys, even if I am older than them. Stairs fold down in the steep bleachers. I hop on the second row and walk the steps, hiding under the coliseum of seats.

Light fights through the bleachers as its obstructed by the wood. The ceiling tucks overhead with its monumental curve, the support beams giant like an elephant's tusks. This is a hidden, tight alleyway that scrunches everyone who walks through it. I'm not claustrophobic, but this seems like something a claustrophobic person wouldn't appreciate.

I begin my journey in the back alley. I take a chance to peek through the white wood. The players continue their practice. Banners hang above the ice, showing off their state championships, dating all the way back to the 1940s. The United States and Canada flag wave above the front room where Max originally was. He's disappeared.

While my eyes still want to soak, I continue forth down the alleyway, getting closer to the zamboni room. The compass cranks to the right as I'm approaching the corner bleacher-bend. Before I can reach the turn, feet stomp above me. Their fingers wiggle through the gaps of the wood. They found me.

"There you are," Max says. I spin around. Max followed me into the alleyway.

"Peek-a-boo," Barrett says. Him and Miles stay on top of the bleachers, watching me through the gaps.

"Dude," Miles says. "Why'd you leave us like that?" The wooden seats slammed shut one-by-one like a line of shutters. Barrett and Miles yanked their fingers back in time before they could've been sliced off. Wooden shutters unfolded and blocked the steps to the seats too.

Light can no longer cast into the darkness. The end of the alleyway behind Max sucks in a little light, not enough to reach around the bend though, but it's a way out.

"Liam," Max says. "Let's get out of here."

"We need the letter," says I.

"I don't wanna be down here right now."

"Head out then," says I. "The letter has to be over here." Max and I turn backs to each other. Max goes steadily to the lighted exit, but his footsteps soften to a pause. I look back while he's amused by a moving object at the end of the alleyway. The white concrete wall pushes out like a thick plate, squeezing our exit into a no-go. The wall crushes into the wooden bleachers and slams into the lower seats, leaving no air to breathe in that bottom section. Then, a second wall beside it pushes out. And a third. It's trying to compress us into paper. "Max."

Max whines over to me. He wraps his arms around me like a toddler, even when we are the same age. It's sort of comforting knowing someone feels protected by my side.

I have no clue how to solve this problem.

"There has to be a way out over here," says I. All the other walls grind out from under the curved wooden roof. I tug Max's arm. We have to hustle before were flattened.

As I duck around the bend, an exit presents itself by the zamboni door, the end of the bleachers on this half of the bunker. A section of wall slides out near its opening while other walls block our way from walking out.

"Max," says I. "We need to crawl faster than we've ever crawled. Stay on my tail." He nods.

I drop to the cold concrete and crawl my hands on the dirty floor. Max keeps behind me as the walls close in, tempting to kiss our rosy cheeks. I shimmy between a triangle of supports. Max hesitates after I make it through. It's a tight squeeze.

"Max!" says I. I reach my hand out. He grabs it. I yank him through the beams, but the closing wall caught his foot. I pull and pull till his foot slips out from his shoe. His lone sole supporter is crushed into a rubber pancake. "Go, go, go." I shove Max in front of me as he crawls to the exit. I slip through the last support beams, back in the shining lights which were dim before but now seem bright.

Max jumps up and checks out the bleachers. "Miles." Miles and Barrett are with us in a jiffy.

"What happened in there?" Barrett says. "Actually, I don't want to know."

"Let's just find this thing and get out of here," Max says.

The hockey stick doesn't point to the zamboni room. It points forward to the other section of bleachers. As I walk to them, the compass turns to the right.

"This doesn't make sense," says I. "It's pointing back to the front of the rink."

"It's taking us in circles," Miles says.

"Can we stay on top this time?" Max asks.

"I'd rather be crushed than seen by these high schoolers,"

says I. Max studies me with squinting eyes. "Just kiddin."

While the four of us stroll on the bleachers, passing the player's benches, the guys on the ice start to snoop on us. We sneak pass the glass. I thought for a moment they wouldn't be able to see me behind the thick glass panes, but then I was stupid enough to realize it. They noticed us for sure but thank God we made it to the other side unharmed, and more importantly, not yelled at.

"Where is it pointing?" Miles says.

The blade points forth, directly at a ladder. The ladder on the wall is protected with a metal cage, in case someone takes a tumble. It leads to the radio booth, perched above the windows of the warming area.

"We don't all have to go up there, right?" Max asks.

"I'll go up," Barrett says.

"No, Barrett," says I. "I'm doing this. I can't lose you."

"I can't lose you either," he says. "Besides, I'm not afraid of heights anymore, and this looks like a radio control tower at the airport. I want to go up there."

"I'll be behind ya," says I.

Barrett climbs the ladder and flips the hatch open to the room. My hands clench to the cold, uncomfortable metal rectangles. I reach the top and pull myself inside. Evaluating the compass, it points directly to the radio desk where Barrett has picked up the letter L.

"That was easier than expected," Barrett says. I smile in relief. It didn't trigger another trap.

"Hey!" a man yells. Out the windows of the radio booth are two coaches standing side by side, staring at us. The head coach aims his stick at us. "Get out of here, now!"

"Go," says I. Barrett climbs down the ladder. I skip a few hand holders and drop down into a squat. Miles and Max copy us into a killer sprint for the exit doors.

"I don't want to see you boys in here again!" he yells.

We run up the steps as the door slams behind us. I bolt through the front doors, leading the boys back into the cold weather. We shuffle to my car and lock the doors behind us.

"Woofta," Barrett says. "He was pissed."

"Dang right he was," Miles says. We spit into a laughter inside the car.

My breath freezes in front of me, signaling me to turn the SUV back on. The car kicks in, but it crackles to its grave.

"Uh oh," says I.

SWEAT

Stranded in my car, we're forced to stalk the high school boys leaving the Memorial Arena. The cold air killed my car's battery. I don't have jumper cables in the trunk, but there are wiser Minnesotans out there who have prepared for this moment. When one of the boys squeals out from the parking lot, my mind triggers me to move. If we don't get out there in time and start asking around, we'll mold into popsicles, and I hate popsicles. They burn the teeth every time. The combination of sugar and ice gets to me.

"We need to get out and ask around," says I.

"Yes," Barrett says. "Let's go."

Max looks at Miles. "You can do the talking."

"I always do," Miles says with confidence. He pinches Max's skin on the chin, puckering up his lips. Max slaps his hand away.

We hop out and track our guys down. Miles and Max start in the front of the parking lot. Barrett and I reach two fellows who open the doors of a rusty truck.

"Excuse me," says I. "Do you guys by a chance have jumper cables? Our car died." Giving Barrett some of the ownership of the car alleviates some of the pressure of stupidity on me.

"No," says the one sitting in the driver's seat. "I'm sure my father has em at home."

"Wait," the boy in the passenger seat says. "Weren't you the guys who got yelled at inside?"

"Uh, no," says I. "Maybe." Barrett scratches his head and turns his face away. Way to have my back, brother.

"Coach was so pissed," he says.

"We saw," says I. Barrett catches another player leaving the arena's front doors. He strolls over to him. "I'm quite used to it though by now. Our head coach turned into a steam engine."

"Yours too, huh?" the driver boy says. "I'd say ours is more of a coal-mine explosion."

The player on the steps is approached by Barrett's strangeness. He stops and stares at him.

"Hi," Barrett says.

"Hi," he says. "Do I know you?"

"No," Barrett says. "Actually, yes. We're the kids that got yelled at."

"Oh," he says.

"My friend's car died. Do you know anyone who has jumpers around here?"

The kid nodded his head. He takes Barrett inside the arena.

"Thank you, fellas," says I. "I think we found someone. I guess the zamboni driver might have them."

The doors to the arena open again. Barrett walks out with the player, and followed by them, the steam engine. The trio confronts me in the parking lot.

"You boys want your truck fixed, you have to speak with me first," the steam engine says. It's not a truck, dumbfounded coach.

Anyways, leaving with no choice, Miles, Max, Barrett, and I enter the arena again. He leads us downstairs and into the coach's room. We sit down in the few open chairs and wait for his dictation. What's he going to make us do for those cables? Or worse, what's he going to do with us?

"You're not going to bury us alive, are ya?" Miles says.

"Or throw us into a pit?" says I. The guys examine me, making sure I'm not going crazy, but only I know the fear I had to deal with already.

"Not at all," the coach says. "I'm Hank, the one who yelled at ya for playing in the radio shack. I'm sure you all remember that moment. And when kids misbehave, especially at your age, the teenaged-thrillers you seek to be, they face the consequences."

"We weren't screwing around," says I. "We actually searched for a missing item of ours, and we got it back."

"What was this 'missing item,'" he asks.

"My notebook," Barrett throws out. "For gym class."

"What was it doing here?" coach says.

"Barrett had to make his own coaching drills for a coaching scholarship," says I. When that came out from my lips, I knew it was a great idea.

"Interesting," he says. "Well, in that case, I could still use your boys' help. I'll go out and jump your car. Just hand me your keys, I'll put you guys to the small job, and then you can be on your way."

"What's the job entail?" Max says.

"You boys will retape all of my boys' hockey sticks and resharpen their skates."

"Are you kidding me?" says I. "We can retape their sticks, but we don't have time to sharpen, what, forty skates?"

"Your fate, not mine," coach says.

Barrett's in as much awe as I am, but we don't have another close choice. "We'll do our best," says I.

"Alright," coach says. "Their locker room is next door." He pushes from his chair. "Got those keys?" he asks. I toss them to him. He leaves.

"I hope one of you knows how to sharpen skates," says I.

"Not me," Barrett says.

"I know how to," Miles says. "I've used our team's skate sharpener twice for high school."

"Alright," says I. "Let's get to work."

Next door is the waiting locker room. It's small, but it's a mansion for this high school team. Although, most kids my age live in houses with granite countertops. I've never lived in a house with granite countertops. Ever. It oddly disappoints me. All I need in life to be happy is hockey though. That's why I hope college can take me there. I want to climb up the steepest mountain and reach the snow-glazed tippy top. It has to have the most beautiful view, but Minnesota has no mountains. Only bluffs and hills and flatlands, and lakes for that matter.

A stick stand holds the teams' candy canes. Half of the sticks have decent tape jobs on them, but the other half appears chipped and slashed by swords.

"We should tape the sticks that need it the most," says I. "Leave the others untouched."

"Yeah," Barrett says. "Where's the tape though?"

"Looks like they're on top of their seats."

"Let's get rollin," Max says.

I steal the roll from a guy's stall. Grabbing a random beaten-up stick, I tear the tape off from the hook and start wrapping the tape from heel to toe. I'm not pulling the sock over the foot. The toe of the stick can stay exposed, although maybe I should learn to tape the toe while you are supposed to shoot off of it. Wrist shots and snap shots should never be shot from the heel of the blade, that's if you care to engage the flex on our stick.

I rip the tape from the roll and finish the first candy cane. That wasn't too bad, but I have many more to go. Max and Barrett make this more efficient. Miles' duty is the long tail. Sharpening skates is like defusing a bomb. Delicacy. Patience. Masterwork.

Taping these twigs with the boys paddles me through a calm stream. Goosebumps force my arm hairs to stand into grass. This is something I didn't receive for a long time. It's peaceful. We're in the eye of a hurricane. I'm not sure how long it'll last, but everything else flushes out from my head. Memories trickle back with the sticky tape peeling from its roll, and the boys focusing on the task at hand. Chester would hang with me on the bleachers, watching the game and taping our sticks. Finn joined us too. I'd be closed in with my dubstep jams, and the other guys chit chatted about the Bantam game that played before us. I guess junior varsity wasn't a thing for us, but it is now. Kielstad is consistent with its accelerating population. Welcome to the suburbs.

There's one guy I missed most though, and I missed him most because I know he's alive. It's torture not being able to see him, talk to him, and distanced miles apart makes it harder.

Checking around the room, the guys work on their task. Miles sparks a skate with the sharpener. Max and Barrett sit in the lockers and wrap more blades.

"I'll be right back," says I.

Leaving the room, I sneak into the coach's room and rummage through a file cabinet. I pull out a notebook. A pencil calls to me on the table. Opening the notebook to a clean, fresh page, I write away a letter of words, spilling out the truth of my emotions, something I will never be able to tell anyone else. I sign the bottom of the sheet and rip the page from its spiral. In the bottom drawer of the file cabinet, I conveniently find an envelope. The letter slides into the sleeve. I lick the glue and seal it. I jot down the sending address, press the stamp on from the drawer, and prepare to leave the room, but steam engine stands in my way. His cold red hands hold the jumper cables.

"What are you doing in here?" he asks. He drops the cables on the table and rips the envelope from my hands. "What's this?"

"It's a letter I wrote," says I. "For my friend."

"Aren't you supposed to be doing something else?" he says.

"I was," says I. "This was something I had to do."

"How'd you know we had this in here?" he says.

"I didn't," says I. "Lucky, I guess."

"These envelopes are for players," he says. "They're for the kids wanting to send their resumes to colleges." He scans the address on the front. "Fort Zumerallo."

"I have a friend in the military," says I. "He's in training."

"You know he can't write back," coach says. "I'm not sure if they're going to allow him to see this anyways. No contact with the outside world."

"I know," says I. "At least I know the letter's out there for him. There's personal things I wrote him."

"Like what?" coach asks. And even though I don't feel comfortable telling him, I do it anyways.

HOSTILES

Gravel crunches beneath a team of boots patrolling along the wall surrounding an urban village. The sun heats their silhouettes on the grass. Tall trees fortify an outside fence around the village. No breeze tickles the tops of those timbers. The crunching of rocks stops as the team lines against the wall. Two-floored, white cement villas tower over the wall. Their organized with blocked windows. Silence strummed up. Only the birds and cicadas sing ambience from the thickets.

Ash is blinded by the sun when he peeks at it through his dusty facemask. He wipes the dust off from his visor with a gloved hand. He's the tail of his squad's line. Coalex, the staff sergeant, waves his hand, signaling them to follow his lead. Ash follows the line along the wall while they approach one of the houses in the block. Two of the second-floor windows overlook the wall, but they're ducking out of sight. Ash keeps his eyes peeled on the windows, but they aren't squeaking for cheese.

Coalex checks around the wall's corner. The coast is clear. He jogs the team to the village's entrance. The tar from the block's dividing road scorches in the dusty yards. Everything's still, but the nearby rainclouds may swing in confetti.

"The overlook house is across the road," Coalex says. "Stay in a line. Hurry with slippers." Ash never assumed his staff sergeant ordering them to be quiet with those words, but it gets his attention every time. He smirks in his mask, but it disappears as the line begins their hushed run. Ash focuses on his teammate's back. His breathing bounces in the mask to his ears, tensing him to run faster before he's hunted.

"What now, sergeant?" Zori, asks. Ash appreciates her presence, not because she's a female but she's tougher than the rest of them.

"We've got to flank around back," Coalex says. "There's a backdoor. That's our entrance." Coalex takes the three of them behind the home. He orders Zori to push the door open when his third gloved finger strikes his palm. She twists the knob and throws it open. Coalex enters the empty room while the third soldier, Gork, follows behind. Ash tracks behind the two as Zori is last inside. The doorway allows the light to sink inside the backroom, but the other rooms space with darkness. Slivers of light come through the edges of the dusty windows, but it's not enough to spot enemy fighters.

"Flashlights on," Coalex orders. "Zori, with me. GA, take the right room. We got left."

From the backroom, there's four more walled-up spaces on

the first floor. The first square is clear. Coalex and Zori scan around the front two rooms. Gork and Ash take opposite sides of the doorway to their room. Ash shakes his head.

"I'm crossing," Gork says.

Gork swings in. Ash syncs with his footwork. No one shines in the gun's flashlight, but a staircase locates in the corner of the room. While Gork confirms the room empty, he signals Ash up the steps. Ash suspects he may worry about this checkup, but he's enjoying this more than he thought. Ash tiptoes up the steps as a dimly lit room settles in silence.

A creaking of wood startles Ash. He trips a foot down a step and readies his finger on the trigger. Gork can't make eye contact with him. He watches Ash recoup as he relaxes his shoulders. Ash steps a foot up and aims to the left. The room's a shape of an L with the rest of the house. The small foot of the L steals Ash's vision while its purely black. He takes another foot up. More of his chest exposes above the second floor. He shakes his flashlight around the room, wanting to lure a mouse out from around the corner. A slam jolts Ash and Gork down another step. Then, another slam catches them off guard, and just to discover one of the front windows is slamming in the breeze, but there wasn't a breeze beforehand. Ash knows that for a fact while he complained in his mind about the sweat buildup under his gear.

"Clear," Ash says. He moves to the empty second floor.

Gork gets to the top and sees the window blowing open and close. "Figures," he says.

Coalex and Zori join them upstairs.

"All clear?" Coalex asks.

"All clear," Gork responds.

The window opens with the wind, then slams shut again. Coalex feels the frame around the window, squinting his eyes to feel for any triggers. Nothing.

Ash lightens in the sun as the window opens fully. Over the road in another house, a fighter aims a gun at him.

"Duck!" Ash says. He falls to the floor as a bullet rockets inside. On the backwall, Gork takes the bullet in the hip. He slides down to the floor and covers from gunfire. The window blows shut, leaving them in the dark.

"Sergeant?" Gork asks.

"Remember?" Coalex says. "We treat you as wounded now." Ash crawls away from the sunlight casting inside as the window opens again. Bullets fly through, penetrating the wall and bouncing to the floor. Fake bullets. "Ash. Take Gork. Help him down the steps."

Just in time, the window closes. Ash wraps Gork's arm around him and carries him away from the impatient window. More bullets whiz by as they walk downstairs. They meet Zori and Coalex at the backdoor.

"Overlook's clear," Coalex says. "Onto the next one. Four-square house." Ash understands he's been through this more than once, he has the layout down to the bone. But the fighters change positions every time for fun. And for the adrenaline.

Sergeant Coalex sneaks them across the open yard of sand and grass between the buildings. No more gunfire.

"You take this one, Zori," Coalex orders.

Zori gives him the three-finger countdown. He flings the door open to a fighter pointing a gun through the doorway. Zori darts the fighter with four bullets to the heart with no second thought. She enters when he falls and steps on top of the fighter's stomach.

"Eh hm," the fighter says. "I'm not actually dead you know."

"Actually, you are," Zori says. She sends another bullet into the fighter's chest.

The room's laid out in a perfect game of four-square, with supporting walls splitting them into four equal sections. Ash scouts outside with Gork, readying his gun for any stunted surprises around the yard. Nothing in sandy sight, but the wind is sure picking up, blowing dust twisters into his visor.

Ash backpedals Gork into the room. Ash's legs fuzz like the sensation of falling in a dream. Knowing there's an open doorway behind him terrifies him, even if this is a training ground. The rest of the rooms are empty. The light from outside carpets the way to the steep steps.

"Never risk a peek up the steps," Coalex says. "Your head will be blown to bits."

Right as Coalex lifts a foot, Ash spots a thin spider web on the first step, paralleling with the stairs. "Wait," Ash says. His foot freezes. "On the step. Look." Dropping his foot back to the ground, Coalex notices the trip wire.

"Excellent eyes," Coalex says. He pulls out a knife and slices the line. Then, he pulls the pin from a gas grenade and tosses it onto the second floor. The simulating gas grenade strobes a green light into the room. They march upstairs to a coughing soldier hiding behind a wall. Coalex shoots the fighter to death. "Building cleared. Let's move out." By the front door of the four-square house, he goes over the plan. "The tree house is adjacent to this one, right across this street. We're going to clean it out before the patio house. That's where the window shooter was located. Let's move." He opens the door. "I'll cover fire if needed. Go, go, go."

The sunlight blinds Ash as he stumbles with Gork at his side into the street. Below his feet on the street, dust swirls into the metal cages of the rain collector. Fingers clench onto the cage from beneath it. The fingers turn into a fist and pound at the loud metal. Ash focuses back on front as he hustles behind Zori to the tree house's street entrance. Coalex sprints across the road while shooting at the patio house's upper window. He receives gunfire back in return. He makes it to the house as they wait on the wall. The door won't open. He nods his head to Zori.

Zori stands back and kicks the door wide open. They break to two different sides as Ash protects Gork in the middle of the house. In front of the opened backdoor, Ash finds Coalex and Zori meeting each other.

"All clear," Zori says.

"Wait a minute," Coalex says, checking the backyard.

Ash squints from the front room and wonders where they'd escape to. Ash whips him and Gork around to the front entrance where a fighter pops out. Ash sprays him down with hip fire.

"Nice," Gork says.

"Cover our backs," Coalex says to Ash. "Let's get to the

backyard. Cover under the wall next to the patio house." No fighters are present on the second-floor patio of the house. They exit the tree house and run to the small desert tree in the corner of the walls. Ash lies Gork down under the tree. "Ash. Zori and I will take the second floor. You cover us. Gork covers you."

"Copy that," Ash says.

"Copy that," Gork says.

"Let's get this finished with," Coalex says.

Ash takes point behind the tetrus wall. He aims his gun at the window which overlooks the outside staircase. Zori and Coalex reach the steps and start their steady climb. The window isn't moving. They reach the top steps and prep for their intrusion. Ash turns his sight to the patio. A fighter sneaks outside. Ash pulls the trigger, but his gun clicks with no burst.

"Gork," Ash says. "I need your gun, now!"

Gork throws his gun to Ash. Ash pulls the sight to his eye and flashes a shot. The fighter falls back onto the patio. Coalex realizes it. He changes his mind about the plan. After giving Ash a thumbs up, Coalex lifts Zori up to the patio. She climbs up top and enters the building.

Ash waits at his point for any action, but he won't be able to do much now. He scans around the village's street, wondering if those fingers were real in that cage. Sweat drips down his forehead beneath the mask. He wishes to take the dang thing off. It's adding to the stress of the humidity. The rainclouds float over the sunlight, giving the village a gloomy appeal.

A door squeaks open. Zori exits the building at the top of the steps. She throws her fist in the air.

"Gork," Ash says. "We did it."

"First try too, aye," he says. "I still got shot."

"You're still alive though, aren't ya?"

"Guess that'll have to do. I ain't happy about it, but it'll do."

Rain suddenly pours down from the clouds, mucking up the sand to mud pits in a quick splash. They don't stick around to eat mudpies for dinner. Instead, they leave the village and hike through the wet woods, but the rain isn't curing the heat. Ash watches the leaves spin in mini circles. The air in his lungs churn into helium, wanting to lift him up to space, but he ends up tripping over the tall grass and collapsing to the ground. He pukes out a mini desert of yellow foam.

"Sergeant," Gork says. "Soldier down." Coalex kneels down to Ash.

"We're still in combat?" Zori asks.

"No," Coalex says. He sets a hand on Ash's forehead. "Heat stroke. When's the last time you ate?" Ash doesn't speak. "Alright. Help him back to camp. Get something into his system."

ICE GARDEN

Pine trees are Minnesota's palm trees. Driving by a pine tree reminds me how spoiled I am living in this great state of untouched state parks and lands. Every time our population goes up in town, I get salty over it. More homes, less land. More cash, less nature. More family, less birds. Nature has its way of reclaiming itself. But my home has done a great job reserving lands to the animals and plants. The snow has its days of stresses; I like the snow, but it's a pain to deal with when the temperature really drops off.

The brothers are quiet in the back while Barrett drives us through St. Cloud. Hank's maintenance skills came in great hands at the perfect time. Guess he's used to it while there aren't a lot of people living up there to help. People are afraid of the cold, but it's not too bad. I'm honestly afraid of the heat. Yeah, I'll never want skates baked again.

Sneaking through the flat-landed city, the puck points us

south to the metro again. Obtaining one more letter will hand us the keys to repair The Barn. But that's if this actually works. I'm not sure Mr. Muckens knows what he's doing, but I suppose his father built the structure in the first place. A master craft for one of the homiest rinks there is.

As much as I'd enjoy another hotel stay with the boys, I'm ready to be back in my bed already, wrapped within my wolf's pelt. I understand the pain of driving for long hours now. It takes up so much of the day and sucks out the remaining fuel I have. I'm worried Max and Miles will nap and screw up their sleep schedule, but maybe I should worry about mine. I'm close to dozing off. The heaters soothe my eyes, and the small bumps on the tires massage my muscles. The sun glows into a giant orb and screens a filter of light over my vision as my eyelids drop over.

My arm bumps into the door as the car turns onto another road. I open my eyes to an entrance. Above the electronic sign are the words of the classic arena. Bloomington Ice Garden. The dead woods hide us from the sun. We drive on the road, alongside of the poles with rounded bulbs on top. The nostalgia hits passing the front entrance to the facility. Every year, we'd have a game here. We'd walk through the doors, found which rink we played in, and packed the locker room.

Finding a parking spot in the lot is like a marshmallow in snow. Barrett quickly gets to an open space, then sneaks in smoother than a spoon scooping into old-fashioned vanilla ice cream. When he parks the car, he hands me the hockey puck back.

"You dropped it in your sleep," Barrett says.

"Did I really doze off for that long?" says I.

"Yeah," he says. "Half a day of driving will put ya to sleep, for an hour and a half."

"Geezes," says I.

"At least you don't snore," Max says. He nudges his brother with a fist. "This guy on the other hand snores earlier than oldies."

"You should hear yourself some time," Miles says.

"I don't snore."

"You do too. We get it from dad's genes."

"Think dad's mad at us?" Max asks.

"Doesn't worry me right now," Miles says. "I just hope we can get out of here in one piece."

"Yeah," says I. "I don't have a good gut feeling for this."

"Why?" Miles asks.

"We have three rinks to choose from," says I. "Three rinks to search through, and it's almost sunset. This place will shut down for Christmas break here around ten."

"We got time," Barrett says.

"Not if we're trapped," says I.

"Or killed," Miles says.

"Should we split up for this one?" Barrett asks.

"Might have to," says I. "With Christmas around the corner, we're going to want to finish this thing before The Barn hurts another team."

"You think it would?" Barrett says.

"It has already," says I. "Shocked a full team of kids on the outdoor rink. A light post fell onto the ice."

118

"When?" he says.

"At the hotel," says I. "I didn't want to tell you guys that night. We were having fun and I didn't want to ruin it."

"Did anyone –"

"No. No fatalities."

"I think we should stick together," Max says. "The puck will point us to which rink it's in anyways."

"Okay," says I. "I'm on board with Max. Let's stick together as a team. That's the only way we'll win."

"Let's do this," Barrett says.

As the sun peeks through the curtains of limped branches, we walk through the doors and are invited into warmth. The lighting is flat, dusty and dim from when it was first built in the seventies, at least that's what the brochure states by the front office window. On the backwall, three laminated sheets point to the arenas. Rink one and two are to the right, and rink three is on the left. Squirts through bantams, it skims my mind that we always had to turn right, either to use the arena with the balcony, or the rink the high school team uses.

"Where's the puck point to?" Miles says.

"Let me check," says I. The stick vibrates to the left. "Rink three, I think."

"It's a starting point at least," Barrett says.

"Yeah," Miles says. "Let's go."

I'm the head of the pack as I lead us past the ticket window. Tall glass panes and two doors present a picturesque view into rink three. Bleachers stair up to the right, the player's benches are on the left. I've always found it odd that a few rinks use frosted glass windows to invite the daylight in, and rink three does just that. The skinny panes allow the darkness of the night to sink in.

A younger team of 15U's play in a game. Small sections of parents control the bleachers. I'm not too fond of attracting the attention onto me. I'd rather not deal with another steam engine, especially at a rink I've played at my whole childhood. Any place in the cities will ban you from its premises, and the countryside will traumatize you from returning ever again. I don't think we'd ever get kicked out but yelled at in front of a crowd is not the path I wanna take.

"We should split up here," says I. "I don't think all four of us should be searching the place in front of all of those people."

"Relax," Miles says. "Who care's what we're doing? Maybe we're just trying to locate a lost wallet."

"I just don't want people looking at us the whole time."

"Same," Max says. "I'm with Liam."

"I guess we can split," Barrett says. "If any of us encounter something, then the other two can rescue us."

"Fine," Miles says. "But there's only one compass."

"It points to the middle of the bleachers," says I. "It's either above or under them."

"Are there locker rooms down there?" Barrett says.

"Yes," says I. "There's a tunnel."

"Okay," Barrett says. "I can check down there."

"I'll go with you, Barrett," Miles says.

"Max and I will take up top then," say I. "Meet you guys

back here out front."

Barrett and Miles go to the tunnel as Max and I head through the doors to rink three. It's a massive tote with towering walls and a high ceiling. We skip every other step to the top platform of the bleachers. The stick on the compass points forth. Continuing straight, the puck slowly turns to the right, then all the way through my stomach. Turning around, I walk forward again as it points the stick at me.

"It's somewhere around here," says I. "Let's see if we can find anything sticking under the bleachers or in the floor."

I squat down and feel my fingers on the top row of bleachers. Something plushy sticks to my fingers. I pull them back and roll my head under the seats. Gum. Typical. Why can't people just spit it out or swallow it?

Two parents twist around and stare at me while they hang upside down. Oh, wait. I get off the floor, brush my shirt off, and wave at them. The two focus back on the game without waving back. How rude of them. I'd expect a friendly hello right back.

"Have you found anything, Max?" says I, casually moving over to him as quickly as possible.

"Nothing but a penny on heads," Max says.

"That's good luck, right?"

"Could be."

"I wonder if they got any hits down there."

As I watch the girls' game, Miles and Barrett stroll through the player's corridor, heading to the entrance door onto the ice. They catch me looking at them. Miles shrugs his shoulders. Barrett points him back into the tunnel.

"Let's check the last locker room in the hall," Barrett says.

"He said it was in the middle though," Miles says.

"Compass' aren't always accurate. I just have a gut feeling it's down here."

"Or something." Miles is right. At this point, expect nothing less than a grizzly bear, a wolf, or a swarm of bats.

The tunnel is tall. Bright at least. It could potentially get away with a ship's hidden passageway if it weren't for the concrete walls and rubber-padded floors. Barrett sure shivers from a draft of wind, pushing from the player's corridor to the back wall. Miles hears his teeth clattering.

"You scared, bro?" Miles asks.

"Nah," Barrett says. "Just cold."

"Whatever you say."

Miles opens the door to the locker room. The door connects to the magnetic holder on the wall. They head inside. While they scan the room, Miles' eyes draw to the stair-shaped ceiling. As uncanny as it sounds, staired-ceilings in a locker room will always be natural for hockey players. And some rinks it works in, others don't so much. It utilizes the space and foundation, but it can equally waste it.

Barrett detects Miles locking eyes with something.

"Miles?" Barrett says.

Barrett observes the ceiling above Miles. He spots an eye peeking through the ceiling. The eye jumps away from the mini hole in the concrete. A click seizes their attention from the ceiling.

The magnet holder gave away. The door closes. Miles hustles over to the door, assuming their fate will be in a latched room. But before he places his hand on the handle, the door vibrates. Clu-clunk. The door bashes open as an avalanche of snow plows into the entrance. It packs the entryway, leaving them with no exit.

"Dang it," Miles says. "I knew we'd be the ones to get trapped. I knew it all along."

"Calm down, Miles," Barrett says.

"No!" Miles says. He darts his index finger into Barrett's chest. "Because of Liam, we're trapped inside. He knew the trap was gonna be down here, didn't he?"

"Liam's decision is going to make our escape more efficient," Barrett says. "And you think Liam wanted to be up top? You know he has social anxiety around crowds, right? His choice wasn't easy to make either."

"Well, where is he then? I don't want to be stuck in here for the whole night."

Max and I drag our hands on the wall, but no gouge or buttons poke our fingers. I sit on the ground with my back against the wall. Haven't been able to relax and watch a normal hockey game in a long while, although, playing a game would be better.

Most of the floor is smooth, but there's a triangle chunk cracked from one of the concrete's gorges. And the compass points right at it. I crawl to the middle and grip my fingertip under its chipped top. I pull from the piece's bill as it slides out. It keeps sliding and sliding like a time capsule meeting the light again. The concrete sheaths out of the floor. I lie it down beside me. I flatten myself to the floor and pry my eye through the hole.

"What!" says I. "What the heck?"

"What is it?" Barrett says. He stops scavenging the trash bin and walks on over.

"Look through it."

Barrett peeks inside. "That's them. Oh my gosh."

"Isn't that weird?"

"Hold on. Let me listen to them." Barrett kisses his ear to the cold floor. "They're arguing."

"About what?"

Barrett fingers me to be quiet. "They're trapped."

"What?" says I. "Are they okay?"

"It looks like it. They're done fighting at least."

"Are they still breathing, Max?"

"Yes. They're fine. Just stuck."

"Okay. Let me try and talk to them." Max slides away from the broken ground. I cup my hands around it and yell inside. "Barrett. Miles. Can you hear me?" Connecting my ear to the concrete canal, I listen for their voices. Nothing. "Hello? Guys?"

"Liam?" Barrett says. I spot him through the small tunnel of rubble. Miles bumps into him. "How did you do that?"

"We don't really know," says I. "The compass led us to it."

"It's not here, Liam," Miles says. "We're stumped on this one. Could possibly be in a pipe or something."

"Possibly," says I. "Or long gone."

"More like not gone," Max says. The compass in his hand redirects us to the right.

"It's pointing at rink two," says I.

"It tricked us," Max says.

"We may have another lead on the letter," says I, yelling preposterously through the floor. The same parents eye me up, eavesdropping on my craziness. It irks me.

"That's great," Miles says. "How are we going to get out?"

"We'll get help," says I. "Don't worry. We'll be back." Before Miles traps us into a typical Minnesota goodbye, taking hours to diffuse, I pop the concrete back into its tube and flush it tight. The compass points the way.

"What about my brother?" Max says. "And Barrett?"

"We'll get them out," says I. "But we're running out of time. This place is gonna close soon. In an hour or so. We need to find that last letter."

"We can't just leave them in there."

"I know, Max. That's why we're going to ask for help. Does that sound like a plan?" Max nods.

While the girls compete with ten minutes left in the third period, the zamboni man stands in front of the opened garage door, watching the game. He appears humble, patriotic for his hometown, wearing an Eagle's jacket with yellow sweats, matching Bloomington Kennedy's team colors of black and yellow and white. As we pass the eye-stalking eagles who've been captivated by my uniqueness, I give them a friendly wave and smile. Oh, how wonderful it feels to make elder eagles confused.

With taps on his shoulder, the zamboni man stares at us.

"Hi," says I. "Um, our friends are trapped in a locker room."

"Again?" he says. "Don't tell me it's locker room four."

"I think it might be," says I.

"C'mon!" he says. "I've fixed that door more than I get paid per hour. I need a raise."

"It's a little more troublesome than the door, I'm afraid."

His eyes dart to the hallway, and his feet follow the line. The zamboni man is pulled into the hallway. We follow him. Around the corner, snow blockades the tunnel, right in front of locker room four.

"I'm going to ask for that raise," zamboni man says.

"Wait," says I. "Can you help us get them out first?"

"As long as you're my witness and reference for my raise."

"Deal. Let's go get the shovels." Zamboni man grabs the two shovels from the garage. "Max. I'm going to go find that letter."

"Liam?" Max says. "You can't do this alone."

"Dang," zamboni man says. After a scoop of snow thrown away from the avalanche, he swipes a streak of sweat away from his forehead. "This is gonna take a while."

"It's okay," says I. "I've been alone before."

I know Max is mad at me for leaving him, but we're running out of time. Christmas break has placed itself under the tree already, the most surprising gift of the year; how fast time has passed, just like my speed on the ice.

Exiting rink three, the compass cuts me through the entryway again and down a slope to rink two. It's a dark and dingey rink. Out the windows, figure skaters practice their Christmas show routines with spins and glides, landing so delicately on the glaze.

The left side of the rink has nothing but a scoreboard, an American and Canadian flag, and the team logos of an eagle and a jaguar while it is a shared rink. The Bloomington Kennedy Eagles and Bloomington Jefferson Jaguars.

To reach the viewing area with barely any seats, I enter rink two through the doors and wander up the closed-in steps. They take me to the upper bunker. It's dark, dingey, and outdated. If the rink wasn't to the left of me, this would be a creepy liminal section. Wrinkly office ceilings rot in the dark while the yellow and blue mini benches rust in the silence. The orchestral music adds to my distaste of the rink. Bending my head over the maroon fence, keeping kids and parents safe up top from falling, are the small benches and scorebox for the skaters and players. The fence is broken up into equal sections by dirty concrete pillars, holding the ceiling up from collapsing on top of me.

It points forward. The compass forces me to look ahead where one of the only working lights shines on the stairs, and to the right of it, a dark corner of blackness. And it's not the darkness that scares me, but space is the absence of light, and I don't want to find myself floating in the midst of the galaxy with no spacesuit. Maybe my hockey gear will do.

The music intensifies with violin strums and cello plucks as I hide in the upper bunker. I pass a pillar one-by-one, keeping an eye out on the figure skaters. The shadows keep me hidden like a secret never to be found. While I'm standing in the middle of the seating area, the concrete wall above the stairs moves out to me, capping the stairs off. The wall behind me seals the top of the stairs I walked up. My feet skip off the floor as it gives a sudden shockwave. The floor tilts from beneath my shoes, down towards the figure skaters. And in front of the figure skaters are the fences sparking to life with lightning volts and buzzing with electricity.

I sprint to the stairs as the floor tilts more and more, angling my body with the support of gravity. Thanks, planet deathrock. I can't exit at all. The walls are too thick to kick through. There are no exits as I can see. I run back to the middle of the bunker. A thought comes across, maybe I could stand on the pillars, but I won't be able to for long. If the floor tilts all the way down like a trapped door, there'll be no possible way. My shoe's friction gives out as I slide onto my back. I slowly glide with the floor's tilt, getting a front row seat to my death, and a figure skating show. Lighting cracks the air from the fence out front, striking the small yellow bench close to my feet. Using the steel for support won't do me good. I shimmy to the side and slip down to the concrete pillar. The floor's probably at a seventy-degree angle by now. The electricity statics like a swarm of stingers, craving to burn my flesh. I should have figured. Eagles don't do well with electricity lines. A typical death for birds caused by human invention.

My back can't handle the tilting floor anymore. No one can see what's happening. I don't want to scream. I swear one of the skater's looked up, but they're all focused on their practice. One of the trash bins leaning against a pillar falls onto the fence. It melts into plastic slime, sizzling into muck. With my instincts and strength, I urge to make a move. I ready my feet on the pillar and my hands on the floor. I launch my feet off from the pillar and swing my upper body away from the tilted floor. I slam my feet into the slanted floor and leap over the volted fence. Before I crash, I hide my view with my sweatshirt sleeves. My arms bang into the ice, cushioning my head on impact as I slide across the ice and into the boards. The figure skaters stop and gasp. While I'm baffled and recovering from remarkable parkour, I smile at everyone, then notice the tilted floor is no longer tilted but locking back into its normal architectural positioning.

After my embarrassing performance, I pull out my hockey compass from my pocket, safe and sound, and leave in a jiffy. The hockey stick points me to rink one. It's playing games with me. The rink is messing with the compass, tricking us into its traps. But it can't last for long. Rink three has to be the place. The last letter is in there, and the compass points directly above the ice, right where a packed high school game takes place.

LINE CHANGE

"Is there a quicker way we can get through this?" Max asks the zamboni man. Max slams the shovel against the hard shell of ice that blocks the door to the locker room. There's no hope that they can reach the main blockade. The only thing they can do now is storm up a clever plan. And clever plans can be the simplest yet stupidest ideas. "Do you have anything we can melt the ice with?"

"You mean like a flamethrower?" the zamboni man says.

"Do you actually have one?"

"I wish."

"You must have salt or something."

"That won't do, but the garage might have something."

Max and the zamboni man leave the glacier, checking around the garage for any heat producers. Buckets of salt are off to the side by the workbench. A hose is wrapped around its holder. There isn't much flashing out to Max.

"Can't we ram the ice with the zamboni?" Max says.

"Not a bad idea," he says. "But we probably shouldn't. This bad boy has injured itself enough back in the days. Can't afford another medical bill."

"That's a bummer," Max says.

"It really is. Especially since an old repair guy used to do it for us for a discount, until he passed away."

"I'm sorry to hear that."

"I can barely remember his name though. It always bugged me. Wait, actually, I think I know it. It's like opening your eyes in pondwater. I can see it but it's too foggy."

"Who is it?"

Back in the locker room, Miles and Barrett bang on the door. Their hands are exhausted and bruised from pounding, trying to make any kind of noise, but no one has heard them. Miles takes a seat on a bench, placing his face into his hands. Barrett sits on a bench perpendicular to Miles.

"I'm not feeling too good," Miles says. "I'm getting lightheaded. Nauseous."

"It's a fricken oven in here," Barrett says. "Here. Hold on to me. We'll get you some cold water from the showers."

Barrett pulls Miles' arm over his shoulders, supporting him to the showers. When Barrett turns the faucet, steaming water pours out, fogging up their surroundings. He turns it more blue for an ice shower, but the heat is dwelling on them.

"What the heck," Barrett says.

"What is it?" Miles says.

"There's no cold water. It's a fricken hot springs. Let's turn you around and go lay on the snow."

Barrett pivots Miles as a red hue glows upon their skin. The rubber floor drips away to a floor filled with lava. The tiles in the shower keep them in a safe box, but it won't be long till the heat burns them alive. Miles collapses to the floor.

"Miles!" Barrett says. "Miles. Are you okay?"

"Everything's . . . waving," Miles says.

"Waving? What do you mean waving?"

"Nothing's . . . flat."

Barrett gently places the back of his hand on Miles' forehead. "You're having a heat stroke. We need to get you out of here."

"I can't."

"Oh, yes you can. Your brother needs you."

"Brother?"

"Max. Your twin brother. He looks exactly like you."

"Who are you?"

"Barrett. Miles, you know who I am."

"Where are we?" Miles asks.

"In a place we shouldn't be. Imma get you out of here." Barrett squats down in front of Miles. "Wrap your arms around me." Barrett grabs his hands and cross them around his chest. "Hold on tight, Miles." He stands up. "Miles, get your feet around my hips." Miles uses his strength and hangs on tightly. Barrett piggybacks him to the edge of the shower tiles, next to the lava pit.

Next to the showers are the benches screwed into the wall, bridging over the spicy hot lava. Barrett lunges a foot to the mini bench, divided from the others for a goalie's changing zone. He pushes off the shower floor, squeezing hold on the jersey hangers. Sweat starts to drip from Barrett's forehead and into his eyes. He swipes them away for his next challenge.

Barrett shimmies a foot out around the mini poked-out wall that divides the goalie bench from the player's changing benches. His foot slides along the wall till it hits the corner of the other bench. He slides his right hand across the wall and grabs hold of its far corner for some grip. As he reaches, Miles hangs onto Barrett's body over the molten liquid. Barrett sends it by shoving his left foot off the goalie's bench while his momentum pushes him onto the other bench. He holds onto the hangers again.

"Almost there, Miles," Barrett says.

The next two benches are easy to cross. He walks from one bench to the other in the corner of the locker room and makes his way to the front door area. The rubber padding is still there, but the edge of it melts away into the lava. It's been creeping from the drain that must have started it all; the water drain that collects the snowballs hockey players chuck at each other from their skates.

Barrett hops Miles onto the rubber platform and discovers the avalanche blockade has been melting from the heat. There's a small crevice between the ice and the tunnel outside of the locker room. As the lava inches closer, Barrett pounds his fist into the ice, smashing small chunks off of the glacier. The lava cascades closer and closer to the front entrance, but as it does, the heat melts the ice quicker, allowing Barrett to break a big enough hole in the ice. He pushes Miles through first before leaving the oven. They breathe in the cold air drifting in from the rink as the door to the room slams shut, sealing its secretive trap. The snow thaws immediately, puddling up a flood on the floor. And behind the snow pile is Max and the zamboni man.

"I'll go get a mop," says the zamboni man.

Max runs over the pile with quiet tears. He hugs Miles whose unconscious from the heat.

"What happened to him?" Max says.

"He needs ice," Barrett says. "A lot of it. C'mon." While they hurry Miles to the concession stand for ice, Barrett senses a hole in the net. "Where's Liam, Max?"

My hands. They're cold. I cup em, blowing warmth to their soles as I sneak behind the parents, yelling at the boys to get the puck out of the zone. In the middle of the walking platform, right above the audience and the player's benches, I slide out my puck which points directly to the middle of the ice. My eyes spot the gold prize, leaning against the metal support beams on the ceiling, right above center ice.

I can't wait any longer. Sure, I'm going to embarrass myself and get yelled at, possibly even thrown out, but it'll save children at my Barn. I can't risk any more deaths. Every single one puts a bullet in my mouth to chew on. With no second thought to hold me back, I wander passed the crowd to the far side of the arena, head down the steps, and with everyone's eyes on the game in the front of the rink, I accidently stumble into the away team's locker room. I remember this odd layout. We played the Eagles twice a year in high school. Once at The Barn, and the other in this rink. This was always our locker room. Through the first locker room door, there's a showering area. And in the room, two rooms fork off from it, leading into two separate locker rooms. It's an organized fortress per say.

Inside the rooms is a mess. Clothes and bags are littered on the floor by the benches. And while it's dark inside, the walls don't seem to even lock into the ceilings like they're supposed to. A flashback pops inside when I played Bantams, and we could hear one of the other coaches talk with their boys, and it didn't sound like a good one. They were losing pretty badly.

The logos on the extra jerseys hanging in the room have a head of a little Hawk stitched on them. Chaska. They're playing the Eagles tonight. Bird against bird. I finally got an idea plopped in my thought. I'm going to get this letter as soon as possible.

ASTRONAUT

Second period has ended for Kennedy and Chaska. The boys hop off the ice as they march behind me to their locker rooms. All of the Chaska guys pile into the locker room I snuck into, but I had to get out of there for this reason. I have one period to do this. Then, they'll be resurfacing and closing the place down for a couple of days over Christmas break. I need that letter, and there is only one clear way to pull this off without drawing a lot of attention. I'm gutsy for doing this.

The coaches for Chaska stroll along to the locker room. I watch the head coach pass by, but I stop the assistant. I feel safer talking to the assistant. Never disrupt a head coach during a hockey game.

"Excuse me, coach," says I. I ended up stealing one of the boys' notebooks filled with calculus equations from their hockey bag, and their name was bolded on the inside of the front cover. Anthony Lawkins. "I'm a prospective scout for a private school, and I would love to have a talk with Anthony Lawkins."

"I'm sure he'd love to," he says. "Can't we wait till after the game though? Usually, scouts don't come crashin in the middle of a hockey game."

"We do things a little differently in our program," says I.

"What school did you say you work for?" he asks.

"We don't like to give out that information right away."

"I understand. Well, let me go get him for you. If you could, make it quick so he can focus on the game."

"Thank you."

He heads into the locker room. I place my forehead on the glass to cool my anxiety down. Only one more thing to do.

Anthony walks out in full gear. He didn't even get time to take his helmet off, and he brought his stick with. Perfect.

"Hey, Anthony," says I.

"Hi," he says.

"Come with me," says I. "We're gonna go somewhere quieter so we can talk."

"Um, okay," he says.

Anthony follows me into the next-door locker rooms, which are empty and closed off from the rink. It's the same layout as the other one they're in, just much more open because there aren't bags lying around everywhere. I take him into a locker room, and we get seated.

"Sorry for talking with you between periods, but I wanted to talk to you about a potential opportunity with hockey," says I.

"It's no problem," Anthony says. "I'm always focused and

ready to play out on the ice. Nothing distracts me from the game."

"Glad to hear," says I. "Why don't you take off your helmet and cool down for a bit here too? I'll probably take most of your intermission here with questions."

"Sure," he says. He drops his gloves and stick on the floor, then unstraps his bucket, allowing his hair to breathe again. While he bends down to place his helmet on the ground, I stand up and walk over to him. I snap my arm around his neck and toss us both to the ground.

"I'm sorry, Anthony," says I. "Please forgive me for this." His hands grasp onto my arms as he tries to pull them off, but he can't in my neck hold. He whimpers as he struggles to breathe, suffocating in his own breath. My eyes water, but I remind myself they could be worse if those kids would have died at The Barn that night. I have to do this for the mission. Anthony elbows me into the side, but the padding doesn't make it hurt too much. He's losing strength. "I'm so sorry. I promise I'll explain later." His arms go limp. He stops struggling. Anthony is deep asleep. I strangle him for more seconds for assurance, then roll him off of me. As quickly as I can, I take Anthony's gear off. I put his lowers on, tie his skates onto my healing feet, strap on the upper pads, toss the purple Hawk's jersey on, and strap the bucket over my head. I'm hoping no one will notice the difference.

After sliding Anthony's body under the bench, I grab his gloves and stick, then leave the room with Chaska hopping onto the ice for warmups. The assistant coach is outside the locker room, searching around for Anthony. He notices me, but I turn my head away from him as he pats me on the back.

"Get out there," he says.

I glide onto the ice, camouflaged in Chaska's grape jerseys. I skate around their zone a couple of times before the referee blows the whistle in commence of the third period. With instincts, I hop onto the bench and stand beside the other boys.

"Anthony," the head coach says from behind me. "Your lines out there."

Immediately, I jump over the boards and onto the ice. The open position is at center dot. I'm playing center for the first line. And right above me is the letter I need to obtain. The puck drops. I smack it back to my defenseman. They pass it to my wingers to carry it into the offensive zone. I don't believe any of the wingers got a good look at my face, but only time will tell. I need to possess the puck.

The Eagles carry it out of the zone. I check the puck carrier as they shot the puck down to the Chaska goalie. He passes it to my winger. We skate up as a trio into the offensive zone. The winger wraps the puck around to the other winger with the curving boards. He one-touches the puck to me from the boards as I crash the net with a one-timer. The puck tings off the crossbar and in. Chaska boys sprint at me as I attempt to skate away from them, but they catch me at the boards in a cramping huddle.

"Nice shot, Anthony!" one of them says.

"Bardownski!" another boy says.

Knowing what to do after, I skate to the Chaska bench for a traditional high five line. The head coach changes lines as I hop onto the bench with the guys. The assistant coach pats me on the helmet. "I'm sure that scout was proud of that goal," he says. My lies eat me up on the bench as I watch the game move on. Above center ice, I can see the letter L leaning on the beam. I need to finish what I came here to do. And I need to do it now.

Our next shift out, I jump onto the ice and sprint for the puck in the offensive corner. I scramble for the puck in between the defenseman's feet. He kicks it out, but I obtain it before his centerman does. I rip a shot on net. The puck rebounds off. The Eagles control it again. I back out of the zone with my line and allow the puck carrier to pass. They shoot it on our goalie. He covers it with a whistle.

Faceoff. I pull the puck back to my defenseman. He slides it over to the other side of the ice. I loop up and receive a pass from my guy. And casually, I flip the puck up and over the Eagle players. The puck barely ticks the beam. While everyone watches the puck flutter, I slide the puck compass from the breezers onto the ice. As the referee blows the whistle from the puck fluttering from the beam, I flutter the compass puck at the letter, smacking it off the beam and falling to the ice.

The dads in the stand yell at the refs that there's another puck on the ice. They grab the compass one, not noticing what it actually is, and hand it to the clock runner. I grab the letter and pocket it inside of my breezers. Over in the glass by the Chaska goalie, Barrett, Max, and Miles holding an ice pack to his head, watch me with a crossed-arms kind of attitude.

"Second times a charm," Miles says.

"It's three times a charm," Max says.

"Not with Liam," Barrett says.

When the puck drops, I let the Eagles win it. I target their defenseman on the boards and nail them into it. I fall onto the ice and roll onto my back. I grab hold of my hand.

"He is such an instigator," Miles says.

The medic walks me off of the ice and into the locker room. I rip my helmet off with my other hand and rest. She puts me through a few exercises as my hand appears functional, but I pretend like I'm in immense pain.

"You might have a fractured bone," she says.

"Sure feels like it," says I. "I'll get my stuff off and head to urgent care with my parents."

"Good call," she says. "Do you need help with your equipment?"

"No, no," says I. "I can do it."

"Alright," she says. "I'll come and check on ya if you aren't out in five minutes."

She leaves me alone in the room. I rip the gear off and throw it into Anthony's bag. When I exit the room, I tell her I'm feeling better. She says I should still get it x-rayed, then I tell her my parents are waiting. When she heads back to her spot in one of the penalty boxes, I rush into the other locker room and find Anthony unconscious but awake.

"Oh my gosh," says I. I sprint to him and comfort his head. "Bud. Are you okay?"

"What happened?" Anthony asks.

"It looks like you may have hit your head on the bench. What's the last thing you remember?"

"I was in my hockey gear. I was playing in a game."

"I saw you got knocked out on the ice."

"What?"

The door crashes open behind me. It's Anthony's parents.

"There you are!" the mom says. She and the father come over by us.

"I found him stumbling in here," says I. "The medic said it was just a blackout from the hit. His hand appears to be fine."

"Thank you," the mom says.

"Who are you?" the dad asks.

"I'm a student from the Eagles student section right out there on the bleachers," says I. "I felt bad for him. I'll get out of your guys' way now. Can I have a fist bump Anthony?" He does. "Get better soon." I leave with a heap of anxiety on my back. Over at the clock box, I tell the guy that was my vintage puck my little cousin threw onto the ice. He tosses it back to me.

In a hurry, I meet the guys at the front of rink one.

"What did you do?" Barrett asks.

"I'll tell you in the car," says I. "Let's just get out of here."

BUTCHERSHOP

"Liam, you should have waited for us," Barrett says.

"You know what kind of trouble you could've gotten yourself into?" Miles says. "All of us, that is."

"I'm sorry," says I. "I was thinking about those kids who almost died at the outdoor rink. I wasn't waiting any longer."

"At least we have the letters," Max says.

"You're right, Max," says I. "It's time to end this monster. For Finn. For Chester."

"For Orson and Shawn," Barrett adds.

I'm driving us back through the countryside to Kielstad. We're needing to speak with Mr. Muckens again about these letters. With the traps we dodged and survived from the trail of breadcrumbs, it'd be nice to know what we're up against now. Like any old, wounded patient, they don't necessarily like to be doctored with if there's nothing to knock em out with.

"Guess who used to repair the zambonis at that rink?" Barrett asks me with a spice of sarcasm. "Chuckle's father."

"That explains it," says I. "A mechanic."

"He worked on a farm though," he says.

"Farmers repair their tractors and toys all the time," says I. "He must have had a thing for hockey then if he cared to repair zambonis."

"Do you think he constructed the rink at the farm?"

"No way," says I. "He loved his farm. The city built the rink for the school, but I supposed he didn't appreciate his Barn being its replacement. I bet he repaired the zambonis for extra profit."

"Then no wonder why all of these places are evil," Barrett says. "He's been to all of them."

"Think he harmed them?" says I.

"With his emotions, he'd drive anything to go haywire."

He's right. Mr. Muckens had poor mental health and no help. Killed his wife even. He brought his burdens with him, probably taking them out on the arenas as he rolled. And I supposed he was probably the opposite of a hockey enthusiasts. That's it. He used the rinks, not only to repair the zambonis, but to hide the haunting letters inside of them. The pieces of the Barn made these traps in the rinks. That's the only explanation. That wood has bloodshed from The Barn, and it's inking into the other arenas, almost possessing them into a different kind of beast. Torture at its finest. Mr. Muckens chose the rinks because he was mad about his own Barn constructed into one.

After the long road trip, Kielstad's population sign welcomes us back home. I swirl around the round-abouts and pull into the lot of Schnickels. We leave my SUV together in the dark, empty parking lot and stroll up to the grocery store. Only one cashier, a younger high schooler, works the front. Maybe Mr. Muckens has left already, but it doesn't hurt to check.

Ms. Esla sure left a long while ago. The bakery sleeps with goodies stuffed in its stomach. Although there's no one to talk to, the guys are attracted to the display of sugar cookies. The way this section just tempts you with its processed artwork is evil. Without a current hockey season in my life, it's going to be tough to stay in competitive shape. What do I have to be competitive for anymore? This killer arena. That's about it. I can't see life without hockey. It's not even living anymore. Life without love is impossible.

I take the boys through the busses of fridges, and in the back of the store is a lit butcher shop with no Mr. Muckens inside. But it appears open to me. I peer around my friends and brother, checking the place out. There's nothing but empty aisles with shelves stocked up. Turning stealth mode on, I sneak behind the meat counter, which covers up to my chest.

"Liam," Barrett says. "You're gonna make us look like shoplifters. Mom won't like that."

"She won't find out, right?" says I. Barrett zips his lips.

In the back, a giant metallic door is cracked open where a cold cloud fogs out from. When I set my hands on the bare stainless steel, I look inside. Mr. Muckens slams his huge, arched butcher knife into a slab of meat. I open the door.

"Mr. Muckens," says I. His arm freezes up. He doesn't look back at me. "We've got the letters." Now, Mr. Muckens pivots around, but his arms are tense. Maybe those are his natural buffed arms. "What could you tell us with preparation?"

"For what?" he says in his deep gutter of a voice.

"To end The Barn?" says I. "We're gonna put the letters back where they belong like you said."

"To end it?"

"Yes. Remember? You told us we can heal it, so it won't hurt more kids."

"The Barn is the only thing I have left of my father," Mr. Muckens says. "That was his creation."

"Please, Mr. Muckens," says I. "Before anyone else is killed. A whole team of kids could have died tonight."

"I'm not letting my father's invention go to waste," he says.

"But the letters, you we're helping us," says I.

"I was searching for those letters!" Mr. Muckens says. "I searched for them my whole damned life! But I supposed it took a few rats like you to get them for me. And now, you're going to hand em over."

"I can't do that, Mr. Muckens," says I. "I'm sorry." I step back from the door, letting the hinges close it back to its small opening.

"You get back here, child," he says.

I wander back to the guys.

"What did he say?" Miles says.

The freezer slams into the back wall as a towering, puffed up Mr. Muckens storms out with rage. His hand suffocates the knife's handle. His buffy arm is ready for a swing. He huffs in my direction with the knife. With no words, the boys and I sprint around the floor freezers and into the food aisles. We run to the front sliding doors, but they won't open.

"What!" says I. "C'mon, Schnickels. What did we do to deserve this?" Mr. Muckens stomps his weight through the breakfast aisle behind us as the store is his ally.

Max runs away from the door. "Max!" Miles says.

"You guys stay here," says I. "I'll go get him."

I pass the breakfast aisle and catch up with Max, but Mr. Muckens doesn't follow me. He stares at Miles and Barrett.

"Hide," Miles says.

"Yep," Barrett says. They agree and cast away from the front doors. Mr. Muckens catches his breath and strolls down the front. Behind the cash registers, the younger girl talks with the police over the phone.

Max and I are stuck in the middle of an aisle of fridges. He hyperventilates. "It's okay," says I. "Max, I got a hiding spot." I push him with me to Ms. Esla's bakery. We duck behind the counter and hide behind cold chocolate pies. "Deep breaths, Max. Deep breaths."

Barrett and Miles smack through the back doors of the store. They hide in the storage room. They're eyes peek through the shelves holding milk and yogurt. Mr. Muckens walks into the dairy aisle.

"Children?" he yells.

Barrett and Miles sit their backs against the shelves. Barrett's teeth shiver in the chilled fright, hoping they won't be chopped to pieces and sold at the counter. Mr. Muckens leaves the dairy aisle and moves past his meat counter.

Peeking over the bakery counter, Mr. Muckens pops around the far corner and into the veggie stands. I hide with Max as he escalates again. I cover his mouth with my hand and lay on the floor with him. Through the pie containers, I find Mr. Muckens calling for us. When the thunderstorm rumbles and the rain waters on the veggies, Mr. Muckens whips his knife, slashing at the veggies ferociously. After releasing his anger on the veggies, He approaches the bakery's display. We're right under him. He listens for a hushed breath in the dark bakery.

Boom. Mr. Muckens attracts to something in the store. I raise my head above the display to find liters of pop bottle rocketing from one of the aisles. Miles and Barrett stick fizzling pills into a liter of cola, shake it up, and chuck it at the floor. The liter rockets into the ceiling. The pop makes the floor into a sticky surprise for Mr. Muckens as he appears at the end of the aisle.

"Go, go, go!" Miles says. He taps Barrett's shoulder to lead their way out of the aisle. Mr. Muckens chases them down.

I pick Max up off the ground. "Now's our time," says I.

"For what?" he says.

"To break out."

Barrett slows down as Miles stops in their current aisle.

"Miles?" Barrett says. Miles tears open a pack of flour and dumps it all over the floor. Mr. Muckens is there again at the aisle's end. He runs at the boys. His foot slips as he falls back onto the floor, shaking the stock on the shelves. He grabs his knife back and limps down the aisle. Miles and Barrett continue to the front of the store where they meet me and Max.

Once Miles grabs a lone grocery cart off to the side, he whips it into the glass of the sliding doors, shattering it to pieces. Barrett hustles over to the young cashier and gives her a hand off the floor. They run outside with the rest of us as Miles breaks the glass off the last doors. The cops speed in, splitting us from a floured-up Mr. Muckens. But in my mind, a scarier man approaches us.

The investigator is here, hiding in the darkness. "Why doesn't it shock me you're in the middle of all of this chaos? I assumed you were here too."

"We had nothing to do with that psychopath," says I. "We asked him a few questions, and then he turned on us."

"Whatever it is, you boys are coming with me," he says.

"No," says I.

"I wasn't asking," he says.

"And I wasn't joking," says I. "We need to end this monster."

"The Barn?" the investigator says. "You sound as crazy as my ex-wife did. But she was right. The Barn revived my son. And you're not taking that away."

"You just watched a whole squirt team get electrocuted," says I. "You're just going to let it live because it saved your son?"

"That place woke my son up from a coma. Reverse science. That arena brings the dead back to life."

"That's funny," says I. "You sound just like your ex-wife."

"And what's that?" he asks.

"Selfish."

I bolt to the car as the other guys copy me. We hop inside and lock the doors before the investigator reaches us. We leave the parking lot, abandoning the investigator in the dust. At this point, no one's safe until we heal The Barn. The cops didn't bother talking to us, and I know the investigator won't speak to them about us. He can't, or I can spill out his psychotic plan with the arena. Blackmail. The whole public can know about his support of the electrocution of a squirt team, his support of his ex-wife creating a sinister summer camp in the middle of nowhere, and his support of studying the spirit of a building. Besides, it's a cold case. He shouldn't be working on it anyways. He doesn't have the right anymore to hold us hostage. Yes, rumors still worry a few of them, but the case is closed.

The time is here. We have what we need. The letters are safe in the glovebox. I drive through Kielstad, down the 30mph road, and roll into the front of The Barn.

Its front doors swing open, inviting us inside.

DRYLAND

All of the lights are on, electrifying the place to life. No one stands on the bleachers through the glass windows, players aren't on the ice skating their warmups, it's dead in here, but yet, so alive. Popcorn hinders through the front entrance, attracting my nose to the concessions where popcorn pops and the pizza display spins with fresh, hot grease dripping down to the metal. The pop machine shows off its lights in blues and bright whites. Candy waits patiently to be taken out of order from all of the children, but not one child begs in line for their parents' money. And music. Music plays in the intercom speakers.

I pass the lit Christmas tree with the guys, having them wait in the concessions area. I peek around the desk in the Library of Skates. No one is working. Before my fear eats me away, I tiptoe around the desk, drafting a breeze by the old shelves of skates, and look around the corner. The skate oven. It rests with its memory of my skates inside. One day, I'll beat the crap out of it. Maybe today will be that day.

Leaving the room, we head inside of the arena. The same song transmits over the big ceiling speakers. I walk up the ramp to the vacant bleachers, sitting in more silence than an abandoned amusement park. No one's cheering, yet there's a brush of warmth against the back of my head. From above, I spot the heaters glowing their red metallic veins. Behind them, on the tippy top of the ceiling, right above center dot, spins the new disco ball.

A rattle of stainless-steel metal grabs at our ears. Miles notices it. I follow his eye of sight to find the zamboni door sliding up. When the door is fully sky high, the zamboni kicks on and rolls back onto the ice. No one's in the seat. Not even the key is in its ignition.

"No one's driving that zamboni," Miles says.

"No one go on the ice," says I.

While I stare at the beast shifting forward for its resurfacing hour, Max pokes at Barrett for an answer, but he knows nothing more than they do. Only I know the horror a zamboni can do to a person. A kid. A brother. The zamboni sloshes clear, warm water onto the sheet, mucking it with invisible blood. It sweeps the sides with the brush while its eyes stare anywhere but at me.

I might be elevating our risk by touring the guys to the zamboni room, but I have to check out the space. I'm hoping Danny isn't trapped in the pit. And down inside the dark cage is a pile of fresh snow. Fresh snow sends a signal to me. Danny. He is here. He has to be. This place is awake.

"Danny's here, guys," says I. "We need to find them."

"Who's Danny?" Max says to Barrett.

"An old teammate of his," Barrett says.

The guys track behind me as I push through the game doors. While I'm watching my feet land on the rubber mats, two figures stand in front of me, way down the excruciating long hallway. A boy points a loaded pistol at another. The boy in the line of fire is Ben. And the hair from the other boy, a bit of a mess, can only be him. That would explain the presence of this place being open. Danny aims the barrel at Ben's heart.

"Guys?" says I. Danny's head spins around.

"Liam?" Danny says. "What are you doing here?"

"We're here to put an end to all of this." Ben checks the gun out in Danny's steady hands.

"Oh yeah?" Danny says. "I had the same idea too." Danny finds Bens' eyes studying at the gun. "Don't even think about it."

"What's going on here?" says I.

"Betrayal," Danny says. "Why don't you tell them, Ben?"

"C'mon, Danny," Ben says. "Both you and I know our friendship wasn't going to last forever. We have different ideals. I want to get a degree, and you want to limp around making a part-time paycheck."

"You stabbed me in the back."

"How did he do that, Danny?" says I.

"New life. New friends. He could care less about hanging with me in front of them. I disappoint him now."

"That's not true," Ben says. With force, Danny shoves the barrel into his chest, pushing him back with warning and intent.

"Alright, Danny," says I. "What's the gun going to do to fix all of this?"

"Make him realize," Danny says. "I know the things he's said behind my back. I've heard him talk about how lazy I've been, how I was the puck hog on the team. He's so full of himself though. It makes me sick. But pulling the plug would feel great right about now."

"Danny. No one's dying tonight. Okay? We've got the missing letters from The Shed. This won't heal just The Barn. It will heal all of us."

"Nothing'll heal our friendship," Danny says. "He's been my only friend since elementary school. Now, I have nobody." Danny's teeth pinch together, turning the pressured bones pink. "I can't believe I trusted you."

"You now feel what I've had to deal with, Danny," says I. "Being alone is my life. I lost my best friends. No one liked me on the team."

"How do you deal with it?" Danny says.

That's not the response I was looking for. As much as it aches in the back of throat, I swallow the anger. "I found new friends. Brothers, actually." I wrap my arms around Barrett. Miles and Max smile at me.

"Heck, we'll even invite you to play pond hockey with us," Miles says. "Have sleepovers like Max and I did in middle school with our teammates."

Danny starts to cry. The gun gently lowers from Ben's chest to his hips. Bens' eyes face forth into mine. I move behind Danny, steadying my steps with soft feet. "C'mon, Danny. Put the gun down. Put it down." I gently push his hand down from Ben's line of fire. I push the safety button on and drop it out of his hands. He hugs me. My brothers watch Danny's tears drip down my back. In front of me, Ben stares at me like a deer in headlights.

A small shake rumbles the lights to sway side to side down the excruciating long hallway. Behind Ben, someone else enters the room. Investigator. I break from Danny's hug while I notice the gun locking to his eyes. His hand reaches to the back of his pants. "What's going on here," he says.

"You followed us?" says I.

"Oh, little boy," he says. He clicks his gun back, ready to fire as he lifts it directly at my head. "I didn't have to. I knew where you were going all along."

"This place isn't what you think it is," says I.

"Of course, I do," he says. "This place is a sanctuary. My son's alive because of it."

"Your son's alive because we saved him," says I. "We're the reasons why he didn't burn to death like your wife did."

"Is that how she went out?" he says. "Huh. You know, I knew my suspicions weren't to be debated with all along. I should have been more confident in myself. You knew all this time."

"Protecting others from the demonic truth is what I do," says I. "I don't like to see people get hurt."

"Neither do I," he says. "Until they invade into my life."

"You'll get sentenced to prison for life," says I.

His eyes stick to mine. "If I can save The Barn, I can save

thousands of lives. My life over theirs. I can live with that."

"You can live with your pity," says I. I spit at his shoes. He smirks, then readies his finger to pull the trigger. His head turns to the side though, almost as if someone walked in. A wolf leaps from behind the corner and attacks the investigator. And not just one. Another one. And another. Three wolves jam their jaws into his flesh, eating him alive. His scream echoes down the long hallway. And at the other end of the hallway, two more wolves stand in a pair. We're trapped from both sides.

"Get in the dryland room!" says I.

The guys turn around. The wolves dash in our direction. We hurry to the dryland room door. Miles crashes through, opening it for the rest of us. Danny and Ben follow inside behind me. Miles slams the door shut. Danny whips out his keys as the wolves bang into the front door. Another wolf attacks the big window. Danny turns the key in the socket, locking us inside.

"What do we do?" Max says. "We're trapped."

"No, we aren't," says I. I try opening the other door that leads straight to the shed, but it won't open. "Danny? Is it locked?"

"It doesn't lock from the inside," he says.

"The Barn," says I. "It's locking us in here." The windows viewing outside to The Shed don't help. They're caged up to protect themselves from flying pucks.

"Great," Miles says. "We're trapped in here."

A whisper of fog leaks out from the huge corner vent in the room. It's also caged over like the window. It's so big, we can easily knee walk inside of it.

"What is that?" Barrett says.

More of it floats out from the cage, pushed from a green-tinted cloud. "Oh my," says I. "It's gas." I pivot to Danny. "Please tell me there's a way out of here." He doesn't say a word. "Get those cages off those windows." I sprint to the window on the right and grasp onto the cage. Veins pop out of my skin like roots of a tree as I squeeze and pull at the cage. Miles joins me, but our strength can't get it off of the wall.

Max and Barrett hustle to the far window. Yanking at it won't work. The gas smogs around them. They cough it out, but it burns their eyes too much. I bang at the cage, yelling for help, but no one's here to do so. Everyone's back at home, relaxing with their families as Christmas approaches. They're all probably nestled around the fireplace and bundled in blankets. Mom's wondering where I am. I know she is.

Barrett and Max come over to us. Danny and Ben wander away from the front door; they attempted to bang at it to scare the wolves away, but they won't move. We're trapped in The Barn's gas cellar. While I'm sitting, I pull one of the letters out. L. And out the caged window is The Shed. It's right there.

"We were so close," says I.

"Are we gonna die?" Max says to Miles.

"No," Miles says. "We're going to get out."

"How?" Ben says. "We're trapped. The Barn wants to kill us. It's going to take us like it did with the others."

"Is that what they were to you?" says I. "Those were my friends. Those were your teammates, Ben. No wonder why none of us could get anywhere with hockey. Our team went nowhere because some of us couldn't man up and figure out how to get along with each other. And now we're gonna die together in the same grave." I slam the letter L onto the floor. It doesn't break, it just bounces near the big window. The wolves stop leaping and stare at the letter. When the head of the wolves, a massive, bulky greyhound, spots the letter, it growls its teeth to a ferocious smile.

It's a risky plan, but I might know how to get us out of here.

POWERPLAY

The wolves imprint their claw marks upon the strong glass pane. We're cubed in between four walls, caged liked wild animals. Poisonous gas pours out from the huge vent in the corner of the room. While the guys huddle together in the corner, I break from them. I cover my mouth and nose with my shirt, masking out the killer clouds of a mysterious lethal weapon. The Barn has never played games with us before. It has no love for anyone.

I kneel on the puck-marked floor, next to the custom-made slideboards. The two long boards were crafted by a couple of our own high schoolers. They're super durable with a great quality finish that you won't find anywhere else. A glaze coats the wood, protecting it from bumps and bruises. We'd slide on these for dryland in the summer. Throw on the classic old socks and practice our strides. We also used the Russian boxes across the room, leaping from one foot to the other on the ramped-up platforms. Sure, got hot in here with those summer days, but at least we didn't get poisoned.

From the side, I see Barrett checking on me. I didn't tell them my plan. We can barely talk anymore with the room's oxygen contaminated. I search the premise of the slideboards. My fingers run along the corners and edges of the wood. Off to the side, part of the wood pokes at my fingertip. I attempt to peel it off, but this wood is too strong. Not cheap. High quality craftmanship for sure.

While there are no pucks visible in the room, nor any object that would make my plan useful, I take the compass out from my pocket and smack at the edge of the wood. I hammer away with puck, shattering the protection plastic off of the front, destroying the cardinal. The wood starts to chip away from the edge. But while I'm beating the heck out of the wood, my motions on repeat cause me to pant for oxygen. I want to taste the cold, clean air again, but only the gas burns away in my throat. Running out of time, my second wind kicks in. The wood is dangling off to the side. I throw the puck and take my fingers, prying the wood from the board. When it rips off, a wooden shard sticks into my hand, giving me the biggest blister in my life. I yank it out, chuck it to the floor, and run to the guys.

"We need to open the door," says I. Hopefully, they heard me while I'm out of breath.

"What?" Miles says.

"Crack the door open, keep the wolves out, I'm going to chuck this out into the hall."

"The wolves are gonna eat us," Max says.

"The wolves don't want us," says I. "They want the letters.

This'll draw us time to escape."

"Let's do it," Ben says.

"Get us out of here," Max says.

"Let's go then!" says I.

We hack up the dust to the door. The wolves jump outside, leaving their slobber on the glass window. When I count to three, they crack the door open. Gas lingers out into the hall, keeping the wolves back from the disgusting chemicals. I lure my arm around the outside wall and whip the wood down the hall. It mimics a lowercase L, which'll trick them only for a second before they realize it's a cheap fake.

The wolves dash down by the investigator's cold body, sniffing the chunk of wood.

"Run!" says I. I pop the door open and book it down the excruciating long hallway. Max, Barrett, Danny, and Ben follow behind as Miles chases our backs. The dryland room door slams shut. The wolves jolt their heads to our running feet. With a bark from the head wolf, they all gallop our way.

Miles checks back and finds the wolves chasing them. "Go, go, go!" he yells. We skip past the locker room and the coach's room. I approach the game doors but continue past them. At the end to the left is the forked-off emergency exit. I crash through with the guys. After the doors slam shut, the wolves bolt into it, body-slamming into the levers and opening them. I lead the boys into a dead-on sprint as the wolves backcheck us. A smile leaks out from my fear. Memories of backchecking drills in high school sneak their way into my head. I know I shouldn't be enjoying this, but it's been a long while since I've touched the ice with my own skates. Maybe it's time to rethink my life over.

We run along the sides of the dingey boards that fence in the outdoor rink. The ice is rough and scuffed, and the light pole is broken upon it, but The Shed brightens the darkness. It's the lighthouse showing us our safe haven. I check into the door. The boys clutter inside the warm house. Before the wolves jam their jaws to the bone, I lock us inside.

The door jumps. It rattles. Shakes. Clanking metal from around The Shed startles us in this small room. In its awkward spot on the ceiling, near the backwall, the heater glows its veins redder than Mars. Lightbulbs shatter above us. Glass glitters down to the floor as the darkness sinks back in. The heater glows an ominous red upon us. Wolves surround us, a couple of them clawing at the giant window, viewing out onto the outdoor ice.

In the middle aisle of the room, right above the center benches, is the carved in injury of The Barn. H-E-double hockey sticks. This is where Mr. Muckens did his work. His anger and psychotic plans grew from this very soil. His farmland was cursed with his depression. He traumatized and ruined his family, creating an evil like no other. He released his anger on The Barn, scarring it for life, leaving it in fury for revenge.

"What do we do?" Barrett says.

"We put the letters back where they belong," says I.

I'm not sure if it'll be that easy, but it's all I got left for a plan. I slide the real letters out from my pocket and set them on the bench in front of me. Vicious barks and growls seep through the

162

walls as the letters are visible in the red glow. I place the H in its spot. The letter flushes perfectly in place. Next, I slide the E inside its slot. One L plops inside, and finally, I push the final L into the skin of the wood. The wolves screech outside of The Shed. The veins of the heater continue to glow.

"Did it work?" Miles asks.

Objects smack into the front of my face. The wall spit out the letters from their marks. They fall onto the floor.

"What!" says I. "It didn't work."

"We need to glue them in," Danny says.

"Where are we going to get glue?" Miles says. "There's no way in heck we're getting out of here alive."

Max cries on the floor, hiding in the middle aisle, staying away from the crazy wolves.

"I'm sorry, guys," says I. "I really thought we could have done this. I don't know why I drug you guys into this. I'm selfish for doing this. I just wanted to get revenge. It took my best friends away. My teammates. I just wanted it to end. But I brought you guys into this. I took your lives away." I wander off into the corner with my tears and hide my face from the others.

Feet sneak behind me, and they're followed by a soft, brave voice. "Liam." I knew it was him. His voice dove into my ears. A memory unlocks from my head, and I notice his face again. It's pallor, but he's happy. We're sitting on the bus together. I struggled to open my bag of bear grahams, he offered to help. He took his small fingers and pulled as hard as he could. The bag exploded in half. The little bears launched all over the bus, falling onto my other teammates nearby. We ducked in the seat and hid in laughter. We even ate the grahams off of the floor by our feet.

A hand of an angel whirled an orb inside of my chest. My feet tingle in adrenaline. Someone magical is with me right now. I turn around to find half of his face lit with the red ominous glow. Max stands behind me with his hand on my shoulder. "We need you, Liam." He implants a smile on me again. I wrap my arms around him and strangle his body into a bear hug.

A gunshot fires outside of the door of The Shed. We hurry behind the half-wall in the middle aisle of benches. A wolf whimpers as the rest of the pack runs away. A bullet strikes the doorknob off. As we hide behind the wall, squeezing together in a tight bundle, the door creaks open. A pair of feet enter the room as a cold draft whirls against my ankles. The shell of a bullet bounces off of the floor as a pair of boots pops in front of me. In the red light, I study the face with a half-grown head of hair.

"Ash?" says I. "Oh my God."

I jump on my feet and hug him. He holds his gun behind my back. "I missed you, Liam. I've missed home so much."

I back from our hug and study his face again, making sure this was real. "What are you doing here? How did you get home?"

"We got sent back home for the exodus," he says. "Christmas break from bootcamp basically."

"Geezes," says I. "I can't believe you're here."

"I'll be leaving again in a week, but I only have a few weeks left till I'm done with camp."

"That's amazing, man." I hug him again. "How did you know

we were here?"

"I went to your house," he says. "Your mom was wondering where you were like me. That kind of answered it. The wolves kind of made it clear."

"Thank you!" says I.

"What are you guys doing here though?" Ash says.

"We're putting an end to The Barn," says I. "Barrett, Miles, Danny, can you go to the zamboni room and get glue or something?"

"Is it going to kill us?" Miles says.

"Max and I will hold the letters in their slots. That should keep it somewhat sane, I hope."

"Letters?" Ash says.

"Ash will go with you guys," says I. "He'll protect you."

"Yeah," Danny says. "I know where wall adhesive is."

With us all in agreement, Ash marches Barrett, Miles, and Danny inside of The Barn. Everything's quiet. The music stopped on the speakers. None of the lights swing. The zamboni isn't ghosting around the ice. Only the wind shackles the tin exterior. They get a tube of adhesive from the zamboni room and bring it back to The Shed. We stick the letters into their place, holding the repairs to the wall, healing The Barn.

INTERFERENCE

Much occurred at The Barn tonight with our presence, yet we stood quiet in the night with no signs of suspicion. I'm inside the tin shed again after gluing the letters in their place, triple checking every room, door, and hallway. The ice got a nice clear coat from the zamboni, the heaters kept the bleachers nice and warm, and the place is quiet again. A little wind brushes upon the arena, but no more twisters shake the foundation. The only blood that could shed in this place is from a classic hockey fight. The Barn has healed, and as long as no one does harm to it, peace will be made. Just like people respecting people, buildings have feelings of their own, and hurting them can do harm. The most haunted places feed off abandonment, vandalism, and pure disrespect. But like people, buildings heal too.

Leaving the main arena, I stroll through the game doors and into the excruciating long hallway. The lights shine my way down the long path, reminding me that The Barn is still awake. It's

brighter than ever with forgiveness. While I pass my old high
school locker room door, right where a giant Knights logo hangs, I
debate on sneaking inside. There is a padded lock on the door
now, keeping outsiders from stealing the players' things, but when
my hand reaches the doorknob, the lock clicks. A green light
blinks on the pad.

I think The Barn invites me inside.

I push the door open to a giant locker room. Stalls cover the
wall and the middle of the room. The boys' equipment dries out
from their recent practices. After Christmas soars by with its joy,
they'll be playing in the traditional holiday tourney in St. Paul at
the historical Doug Woog Arena. We didn't really win the tourney
through my years, but it's always a blast to play different teams
from around the cities.

On the stalls, I read a few unrecognizable names in the front.
But in the back, the fancy nametags list the players I do know.
Jake and Charlie, the senior defensive pair this year, sit together in
the back, right beside their senior goaltender, Thomas. The boys
have a good season going for them right now, not sure if they'll
make it to state being a double A team now, but it never hurts to
try. The worst feeling in the world is knowing you could have
done better after you've already lost.

It's strange to think my mother coaches the high school team.
A female coach running a boys' team is a rarity never seen before,
or at least I haven't seen it done. She's doing an awesome job.
Honestly, a figure skater, male or female, for a skating coach
would be epic. It's insane how much technique could be tweaked

for better feet. But mom has a strong desire to build this team from the dirt and compress them into stones.

Heading out of the locker room, I pass the dryland room and approach the corner to the concessions area, but the imbalance is preposterous. Investigator's body isn't here, but one of the emergency doors to my right is slit open. Outside the doors, a wolf pulls the remains of his body passed The Shed and into the woods. It left a little of his blood stains in the snow, but blood near a hockey rink? C'mon. That's normal.

Back inside, the rest of the guys coup in the concessions area. Ben and Danny are inside of the stand, hugging it out by the candy display. Danny's hurt, but Ben releases his arms from him. Danny continues to hold him in a hug, so he wraps them back around.

"I'm so sorry," Danny says. "I hope you don't see me differently with all of this."

"You never changed," Ben says.

"You have though," he says.

"It's college. This is when we transform ourselves into something greater than we ever believed. This is when I can chase my dream and make it happen."

I sneak over to the other guys. While Barrett and Miles chit chat to each other, I eavesdrop onto Danny's and Ben's conversation. "What's you dream?" Danny asks. "You never told me you had one."

"To be rich," Ben says. "I'm going to own a mansion."

"Oh," Danny says. "I knew that."

Same here, I think to myself. Ben never cared about hockey

that much either. He's always been in it for the fame and fortune, and it seems college doesn't change everybody.

"Will we ever hang out like we used to do?" Danny asks.

"I'll see you around," Ben says. "Maybe next summer after school, we'll do something."

Ben leaves the room. He tells us he's leaving and heads out the double set of french doors. I wander into the concessions by Danny who sits on the counter. "He's not gonna hang out with me, is he?"

"You never know," says I. "Maybe a few times. But never count on it. He might be a different person than you thought he was in high school."

"I feel used," Danny says.

"Welcome to my life," says I. I pat him on the back. "You can always hang out with me." Danny swipes the snot from his nose and hops off of the counter. Without another statement from him, he grabs a chocolate bar, tears it open, and eats it leaving the room. "Gotta love trying anyways, right?"

Danny rebounds inside the room again. Before I hop off, he stops in front of me. "Liam," he says. "The Barn isn't done yet."

"The Barn?" says I. "What do you mean?"

"Kiv plans on selling it to the city."

While my stomach rumbles with a long foodless day, we drive over to Carbone's for a late-night meal, the night before Christmas Eve. We're sat down in the middle of adults and late-staying families. The arcade machines are off to the side. Flat screens play sport replays and a Wild hockey game out in Los

Angeles. Our pizza cooks in the oven while we satisfy our time with glass bottles of root beer.

"Why does Kiv want to sell the rink?" I ask Danny.

"Well, after a whole team of squirts we're almost killed from a falling light pole at the outdoor rink, he fears all of the deaths will bring him a lawsuit," Danny says. "That was his last straw."

"I hope he doesn't put the burden on himself," says I.

"He doesn't," Danny says. "He's just grumpy about it all."

"Time for retirement," says I.

"He's like thirty, dude."

"Oh. He's halfway there. He'll be fine."

"How are we going to keep The Barn?" Barrett says.

"Yeah," Miles says. "After all of that hard work I put in to save this farm barn, I hope it doesn't burn in the landfill."

"Kielstad needs a rink," Max says. "They aren't going to rip away the only rink in town just so the boys and girls have to practice and play in another city."

"Max is right," says I. "But they might move the rink somewhere else."

"Or even worse," Barrett says. "Renovate it. I'm not sure if The Barn would like its history torn down."

The waiter carries our pizzas around the bend of the bar. Before he places them on our table, I release the words. "I might know someone who'd buy the arena."

After eating with the boys and saying our farewell to Danny for the night, I drive Miles, Max, and my brother, Barrett, back to my house. We grab our styrofoam containers of leftover pizza and rush into the warmth of my home. Nothing beats a long trip with the ending destination of your own bed.

I close the door behind the guys.

"There you are," mom says, popping out from the kitchen. "I was getting worried about you guys." She notices the twins. "I don't believe I've met your friends, Liam."

"Miles has the cross necklace, and Max is the other one," says I.

"Liam!" she says with a chuckle. Then, she leans into me with the mom tone. "Be a little more polite about it."

"They're cool with it," says I.

"Leftovers for me?" she asks.

"Yep." Barrett and I hand her two containers full of pizza. "Merry Christmas."

"What?" she says. "It's not Christmas yet though. This doesn't count. I'll expect a present from each and every one of you under that tree by Christmas day." Before she heads into the kitchen to put the pizza in the fridge, she winks at us, making sure we understood the joke. Although, I didn't buy her a present this year.

Not yet anyway.

DELAY OF GAME

It's a sunny Christmas Eve. The cold hasn't winded away, nor has a warm front hit us for a long few months. I'm driving on the freeway to the cities, not only to shop for my mother's gift which I haven't been able to search for, but to drop Max and Miles off at their car, left behind at Homerun's parking lot. They'll need to make their journey back home, leaving enough time to discuss things with their dad before Christmas Day. The brothers don't look thrilled. Max stares at the windows, watching other cars roll by. Miles fidgets with his fingers, scratching his arms and head and picking at his nails. I suppose years of historical bruises may scar them for the rest of their lives.

We're tired driving on the road, and I think Barrett will drive us back. I'm sore from sitting in this seat for hours. The dash is loaded in my memory. I can feel when the car's cruising too fast down the road without checking the speedometer.

Moments later, I turn into the parking lot and pull next to the twins' vehicle. We hop out and grab their things from the trunk. Max drops his luggage and wraps his arms around me.

"I don't want to leave," Max says. Miles looks at me, not knowing how to comfort him anymore. I'm sure he's done as much as he can, but he must never stop. "Can I stay with you?"

"I wish," says I. "I don't know if we'll have enough room. And I'm sure your father loves you more than you think."

"I don't think so," Miles says. "Never has. Never will."

"You guys will always be his sons," says I. "Let me give ya a tip. Do something beneficial for your father, something he'd love. Make him care for guys. See if that changes his perspective."

"Like what?" Miles says. "Wrap a Christmas gift for him?"

"That's exactly what I'm saying," says I. "Wrap something of value for him that'd he appreciate."

"We can buy him poker cards," Max says. "He never stops talking about how good he was at poker in his days with our neighbors and friends."

"That's perfect, Max," says I. "And affordable. Get him a poker table too while you're at it."

Max hugs me one last time. Miles holds his fist out. I bump it with mine. They head inside of the car, buckle up, and as they roll away, Max watches me fade as the distance between us grows greater, but yet, never less. We'll always be connected in memories. And we don't live too far from each other.

I can tell the brothers are scared. They don't want to head home and live the ordinary life they're used to. But both of them play hockey down there in Mankato, training for more years with

Juniors. That's something I never had the opportunity for. I'm still in the age limit to do so, but why didn't I ever get the chance to play? Senior year destroyed me, and the memories still haunt me.

Barrett and I drive to the mall. When I shift the car in park, we walk inside the entrance with no idea what to shop for. My mother's not the easiest to think of when it comes to gifts. Maybe she'd like something for the kitchen. Nah. That's too expensive and puts her to work. Could a simple candle and basket of goodies surprise her? Nah. That doesn't satisfy me either.

While it's toasty inside, it's calm rolling around a peaceful mall on Christmas Eve. I'd expect more of a hassle around here, but most of the parents bought their children's gifts by now. And it's lunch time. The mall closes in a few hours too. Shops of knick knacks, clothes, technology, and shoes all show off their displays to us, but nothing screams out for my mother.

A sportsy shop halts me after we whiff past the food plaza. My eyes catch a hockey jersey hanging in the window. A last name of a professional hockey player is stitched to the back with their number. And it hands me an awesome present idea for mom. I know she'll like it. I explain my idea to Barrett.

"Is that a good plan?" says I.

"Yeah," he says. "It's perfect."

"It's not too cheesy?"

"Not at all."

With that clarified, Barrett and I purchase the goods and leave the shop. We exit the mall and open the doors to the car. Barrett accepts the offer to drive us back home. And as he speeds onto the freeway, I dangle my head to the side, the sun casting its warmth upon my skin. The low heaters keep my feet warm, and when I close my eyes, I imagine myself on the school bus again, riding to the arena, sneaking in a little nap before game time. Bumps on the road, and the ambience of other rumming cars, all becomes a blur in the background.

All I want for Christmas is hockey to be back in my life. I understand it can't be wrapped in a box, but it can unveil itself in real life. I don't have anyone to help lead the way. Hopefully, a miracle spins up for me. I've seen it done before with others. And of course, the one thing I want is the toughest to receive. If I can't earn it, then what is life? Pointless. No life without love.

Back home, Barrett scouts the inside of the house. I wait behind the car with the trunk opened, watching him spy out the first floor. He waves me down to come over to him. I take the hamper of gifts, covered with a dirty blanket, and hustle through the front door. Barrett shuts it and hurries with me to my bedroom.

"Alright," says I. "Let's wrap it up."

After wrapping the gifts, we leave my room. Down the hall, water pours inside of the bathroom. Mom must be showering. Heading to the first floor again, we crash on the couch as the news is on. It couldn't have timed out any more crisply than this.

The tagline displays the title of a missing investigator found in the woods outside of Kielstad. A boy, close to my age, stands on camera in a live interview.

"Your father was found with attacks from local wolves, and your mother's body had never been discovered," the reporter says.

"How do you feel with all of this? I can only imagine it's hard."

"It is hard," Clayton says. "It's hard to wrap my mind around all of this. It finally happened. I'm free!"

"Am I hearing this right?" the reporter says. "Clayton, what are you saying?"

"My parents were psychos," he says. "I like my stepdad."

BOWS OF LACES

The morning's light wakes me up earlier than ever. My adrenaline immediately rushes as Christmas blinks in my head. I throw on comfy clothes, pull on my slippers, and slide on the floors to the Christmas tree. No gifts. Not one. Only ornaments and lights glimmer on the tree. Mother's gift is still in my room for a surprise, but not one bow lures my eye.

Barrett runs up the steps from his room in the half basement. When he reaches my side, he's confused as I am.

"I shouldn't be needy," Barrett says, "but usually there are presents under the tree morning of."

"There usually is," says I. "Mom never forgets. She must've slept past her alarm."

"No, I didn't," mom says, standing behind us. "We're spending Christmas somewhere else this year."

"What?" says I. "Where?"

She holds up keys looped around a ring. While it doesn't

answer for itself, Barrett and I grab her gift and set it in the SUV. We follow my mom on the country roads, rolling over the hills and curving around the snowy crop fields. Rolling down the 30mph road, we halt in front. My mind can't intake this all at once. Barrett hurries out of the car and opens my door for me.

"C'mon, Liam!" he says. He pulls me out, galloping my legs with his to the front where mom unlocks the double set of french doors, inviting us inside.

"But how?" says I. "How did you know?"

"You don't think the high school hockey coach in Kielstad would hear about it?" she says.

"You bought it?" says I.

And with a nod of her head, Barrett and I rip through the unlocked doors and discover the gifts under the Christmas tree. We place mom's gift beneath the pine needles too. Over to the side, bodies hide in the dark. With a flick of the lights, a bunch of goons surprise us. Thomas. Jake. Charlie. Ash. They all came for Christmas day.

"Merry Christmas!" Jake and Charlie say in sync.

"I can't believe this," says I.

I go and strangle my friends in a group hug. Barrett stands back, breathing in the emotions of love and exhaling support on my shoulders. He even drops a tear down the side of his cheek.

"Can I open the eggnog, now?" Thomas says.

"Yes, please!" Ash says. "Do it, now. I've been quenching for it all morning."

Plates of gingerbread cookies, cheese and crackers, and warm pancakes rest on the table. We grab paper plates and dig into the treats. The eggnog was pre-poured into plastic cups for us all. All of us sit together around the put-together tables in the concession area. The gifts await to be open as we smack on our breakfast.

"Who cooked these?" says I.

"I did," Charlie says.

"Dang," says Thomas. "You are skilled at something."

Jake explodes eggnog from his mouth all over the table, spraying me and Ash with his backwash. We all laugh, reminding me of the times we had a pre-game meal together, the day before a big game. I know to take in this current moment while they won't last in the future but will vanquish in our past. Living in the present is most important in life because you'll never know when something can be ripped from your hold.

After Christmas breakfast, we unwrapped our gifts. Mom got us all something, even the other boys who came. Barrett and I opened an air hockey table and floor hockey nets. The other boys got cool hockey lanyards, clothes, and their own floor hockey sticks. Mom hands us a huge gift all together in the end. When we tear the wrapping off, our mouths drop to the floor. A laser tag set. Laser tag in The Barn. That's a definite must.

At last, mother's opening her gifts from Barrett and I. She tears it open, and as we expected, she can't hold in her emotions. She pulls out the coaching jacket, pants, whistle, a whiteboard, markers, and a picture of her, dad, and I in a custom hockey frame. We also snuck in some treats inside too, mimicking the colors on the ice of red licorice, blue fish, and white taffies.

While the boys and I craved for laser tag, Barrett and I grabbed other players' skates in the high school locker room and threw them on with the other boys. With one puck, we played a game of hockey in The Barn. The ice is crisp, clean, and smooth. I'm skating on the heavenly clouds. Although a few teammates don't own their heartbeats anymore, I feel their ghostly presence out here on the ice with us. My chest is like an air balloon, rising with greatness in this fresh air. Their spirits cause my skin to tingle, not to goosebumps but a comfortable chill.

Oh, the good ol days when we'd be ran in practice by the captains. All we'd do for captain's practice was scrimmage, and that was the best way to get to know each other and stay in decent shape. It'd be late at night. Some of the nights, there was a football game to the field right by The Barn here. And while everyone focused on the football game, us hockey players enjoyed our time on the ice. Most of us at least. The main guys would skip of course because their appearance at the games were more important than their teammates. But I tried to let that cast by and not bother me. The worst I could do is stay hooked with others' problems. I have goals of mine to score. As amazing as Christmas is today, my mom owning The Barn, reunited with my friends, and eating Charlie's tasty pancakes, I still didn't receive what I need in life.

When can I play on a hockey team again?

THE ARENA

Kielstad revives itself to normality again. Mr. Muckens was arrested with lighter charges filed against him. The cold case is dead while no investigator attempts to open it again. The Barn is healed, and welcomes are presence inside. Mom went back home a while ago to catch up on some sleep, but she gave me the keys to the rink before she left. And the boys send the message to me with their eyes. It's laser tag time.

We load on our vests and charge up our guns. I grab a loading and healing checkpoint on the far side of the arena, right inside the zamboni room. Miles sticks the other checkpoint in the concession stand. Barrett, Ash, Thomas, and I are on team red. Miles, Jake, Max, and Charlie are on blue team. I run over to the clock port and press the play button on the old MP3 player. A voice begins the countdown of play across the arena. I hurry back to my squad in the zamboni room. While Ash pulls on the chain to open the giant steel door, I lie my phone on the work shelf. It shows our names, points, and the teams' score.

Techno music commences us to leave checkpoint and to run to our spots. Ash and I take the bleacher side together. Thomas and Barrett break from us as they split towards the corridor behind the team benches.

"The hallway's gonna give us too much exposure," Ash says. "We need to find a way to sneak behind their backs."

"Backstab them," says I. "Great plan."

"But how? We'll be spotted on the bleachers too."

Our only way is to cross the exposed areas or wait out the enemy. But I'm assuming the other team won't pressure either. Wait. There's a storage door that blends in with the sides of the bleachers. Kiv used the space under the bleachers to store concession goods, rink equipment, and other junk he hoarded. But it's locked. Oh, yeah. That's right. I own the keys.

"Follow me," says I. "What if I knew a way?" I smile as I slip out the keys from my pocket. I unlock the hatch and squeak the door open. "After you." Ash smirks. This isn't cheating but using our resources wisely.

I close the door behind us. I remember the older bleachers when I was as little as a mite. The bleachers had huge gaps in them. People would lose money, and kids would drop candy, all of it scattered onto the floor. I used to crawl under the bleachers and scavenge for coins, anything of use for those candy machines in the front. But now, the modernized bleachers darken the back here. No one would know there's usable space beneath them.

Suddenly, the lights power off. It's pitch black, but our guns and vests brighten the space red. Blue team flipped the switch from the Library of Skates.

"That'll do," Miles says.

"We're so gonna dominate," Charlie says.

"Let's get em," Jake says. "Max and I gonna watch the hall."

"Okay," Miles says. "Charlie and I can stake in the mini hallway. We'll watch the front area too."

Barrett and Thomas tiptoe with their guns pointed forward as they make way behind the team benches. The techno music drops into another adrenaline rush as they keep pushing forth. They await a jump scare, but there aren't any blue lights shining on the wall anywhere. Thomas surveys the backwall of the benches incase a player overlooks them, sniping them out of a barrel, but no one jumps out.

"Campers," Thomas says. "I knew it."

"Playing it safe," Barrett says. "Smart. They're luring us in with slow game."

"Good thing we're patient."

"Goalies are patient?" Barrett asks. He slaps Thomas' arm for a good ol sieve joke. Thomas understands for sure, and he actually likes a newer joke for once.

Ash and I approach the other door, but it's locked from the outside. Good thing there are old stools back here. We stand upon them and crawl over the door. We hop onto the cold concrete floor and hide behind the private meeting room wall. Behind the wall are the doors to the concessions area. No one in sight.

"Wait," Ash says. "Near the front in the hall."

Through the glass windows that view into the welcoming area, a blue hue glows upon the far wall. "Blue lights," says I. "Let's get em."

"Wait. If they split into two groups like us, the others would be on this half."

"Long hallway?" I ask.

"Or the sharpening room?"

"As long as they aren't camping in the concession stand at checkpoint. Cheap move to replenish their health immediately."

"Smart move if they did."

"Not enough to outsmart my friend."

Our gear clicks a little as we hustle to the doors. Lights still shine to the left through the glass, but nothing on the right side. Ash leads our way. Quietly and quickly, our feet walk on sand to the Library of Skates. No one's inside. No one hides behind the counter or in the closet with the skate oven and sharpener. We wait patiently in the corner and spy on the two blues from across the room.

"Do we shoot?" says I.

"Not yet," Ash says. "They're still out a ways."

Charlie perks his gun behind the wall of Locker Room One. Miles lies on the floor by Charlie's feet, pointing down the mini hallway to the arena's closed door.

"I see red," Charlie says. "Two of them. They're approaching the door."

"Ready on my go," Miles says. "They'll see our vests through the window. We gotta shoot when they open it." The door slams open against the wall as Barrett and Thomas storm in. Both pairs spray each other with colorful bullets. Miles is shot from Thomas' bullet, then Thomas goes down from Charlie's shot. Miles runs to the reloading station as Charlie attempts to cover, and he does. A laser strikes Barrett in the chest. Barrett and Thomas gather themselves together and run out the door. They must dart their way back to checkpoint to replenish their health.

Charlie leaves Locker Room One, guessing he'll have time to help his other teammates. He runs to the concession stand where Miles replenished himself at blue's checkpoint.

"Should we join the other two and check up with them?" Charlie asks. Miles spots Barrett and Thomas still at the other end of the arena, reloading themselves at checkpoint.

"Yes, but quickly," Miles says. Ash and I discover the two heading into the excruciating long hallway with Max and Jake. Miles spots them in the dryland room where the door is held open with a sandbag. "How are you two holding up?"

"Fine," Max says.

"Haven't seen one guy yet," Jake says. Then, his eyes shine brighter than the sun.

Ash and I spray the guys down to their doom. Now, we're in the lead. Red team's gonna win this.

"Woo!" says I. Ash and I high five each other in a snap, right in the doorway where team blue can see. Before they chase us out, Ash and I sprint back to deployment to reset and re-dominate.

My phones reboots with health and ammo. We're leading on the scoreboard. Charlie and Thomas already made their move back to the front of The Barn.

"Shall we go get em again?" says I.

"Let's do it," Ash says.

ROUGHING

I'm stoked the holidays aren't over yet. Christmas break isn't only about the Christian holiday but our planet circling around the entire sun. New Years is on its way. While I'm happy with who I am, my focus has to be tweaked. The time ticks away every second, and every second I lose is another second without love. The time builds up, and it'll eventually overload my happiness, spilling into a depression flood. Switching my focus pulls hockey back into my life, and balance is the importance of it all. Brilliance can't occur without failure, and happiness can't be achieved without depression. Fighting for what I believe in helps me and my motivation with hockey. I'm gonna take it back into my hands.

Dad would love watching me hold a candy cane in my hands again, shooting the biscuit into the net. And not the net that protects the fans from getting nailed by a puck. I'd smoke that cookie between the crossbars, right through the swiss cheese standing in net. But the problem confronts me. The conflict isn't where the train'll take me, but where the frick is the train station in the first place? Where's the starting point? Who's to ask? And it isn't a normal station. It's a ghost train. No one likes to talk about it. It's this giant secret that only the wealthy trap inside their bubble. Outsiders should never know what happens on the inside, or else they may take power over one another. Perhaps it's a compliment that no one wants to show me the way because they're scared of the power I hold. But what is that power?

For her support, Barrett and I travel to the sinister gossip shop and visit Ms. Esla. The morning after Christmas day can only mean she prepared freshly baked donuts. An old lady's craft dominates the rest of the processed crap on the shelves. Her donuts slam with sweetness, yet they contain healthy, wheat ingredients. Selecting donuts from the display may steal time from the other customers while Barrett and I are choosy.

"Too many to choose from?" Ms. Esla asks. "Here. Let me help you." She points her crinkled finger at a blue frosted one with sprinkles and cream in the center. "This one here'll stuff you up quick with sweetness. But if you're feeling chocolatey, the brownie bite donut will satisfy those tummies."

"I'll do one of each," says I.

"I'd like to do the same, Ms. Esla," Barrett says.

"Oh, yay!" she says. "I'm proud I could help. I'll even sneak in a snickerdoodle cookie for you young, handsome boys. It's on the rocks."

Barrett leans his wet lips into my ear. "I think she means it's on the house."

"She worked in the military," says I. "They mean the same."

Grabbing our delicious donuts in their baggies, we tip Ms. Esla and leave Schnickels. While we were there the other night, we roll on over to The Barn. Barrett and I collected jerseys from our fallen warriors and plan to hang them in the arena. They're jerseys are in the trunk, sitting in a clean box; Finn, nineteen stitched to the back of his jersey; Chester, seventeen on his. Those numbers stand for them in this Barn. At least for remembrance. They were heroes in my heart. Hanging them near the flag dedicates our love to them, and every time that National Anthem plays, they'll wave with the flag to us, right there in The Barn.

We arrive at the rink. Unlocking the double set of french doors, the lights power on, and we get to work, hanging those jerseys up by the flag. Teams play later tonight here, older ones of course. Peewees, Bantams, U-sixteens, Christmas break is weak without a game of hockey in the mix. Many rinks host Christmas tourneys afterwards, but this year, on quick notice, my mom setup a donation event where me and my teammates collect gear for the young who can't afford it. Anyone who wants to play hockey shall have the opportunity. I wish that's how it ran at my age.

Until another world war occurs, I'm afraid we're all stuck in our own greed. We seem to forget the importance of accepting others. Of course, the older the hockey leagues get, the tougher they'll be to try out for, but is there anything wrong with handing out more sustainable opportunities who don't get drafted? Maybe I just need to accept the fact that I'm not good enough. After all of that hard work in high school, having the best weightlifting records, speed, and dedication on my team, maybe I'm still not reaching that level of power the scouts are searching for. Barely had scouts watching our team in high school anyways. Our team wasn't heading to state anytime soon. My guys never gained that level of dedication to it all. Half of them skipped out on team workouts, and friendships blocked the rest of us out from merging together as brothers. Only a team with epic connections with a game. Our team founded from lines stringed together as a trio, but the strings could never connect to produce a stronger web.

When we were done hammering the jerseys into the wall, I threw myself away from Barrett for a second and wandered into the high school locker room. I walk past the others and stare at my old stall. Another kid occupies the space with his gear. The room invites me with hominess still, but my hearts torn. Life was easy in high school because I engaged with what I love most. It ran away from me, and I'm not positive if I'll ever catch up with it again, like a small lost dog ripped from its feet by an owl, snapped into a scrumptious scum of death. No more love lingers from the dog. It's only a fluffy load of protein left behind for mother nature to decomposite and bury into the soil, allowing the trees to drink its blood as tropical fruit punch.

As I leave the locker room, my train of thought derails into nostalgia. Last night was one of those moments I'd want to travel back in time to. Ash flew back home from training. Miles and Max were at their happiest place. I saw Jake, Charlie, and Thomas again. Spent Christmas with mom and the boys. And it was the day I received the biggest gift ever. Although it's a great gift to have The Barn, I continue to dream and mope about playing competitive hockey again. But Miles and Max, I wonder how they're currently playing. They're good players, but we're about the same with stats.

Speaking of, Miles and Max waited the night out at a hotel. Miles sent me a message, informing me they needed another day of preparation. Miles is nervous like Max, but he hides it from him, attempting to keep Max from inducing an anxiety attack. They predict their father is prepared with the belt. At least their father breathes above ground, I wish mine did. My father would've supported me on the right tracks with hockey, but I'm on my own.

Miles parks on the curb to their house in Mankato.

"Do we have to go inside?" Max says.

"Yes," Miles says. "He's our father."

"He's gonna yell at us."

"Not on my watch." Miles reaches his hand and feels for something on the back seat. "Where's his gift?"

"By my feet," Max says.

"Do you want me to hand it to him?" Miles asks. Max nods. "Okay. Let's wait till the end though."

They close the doors softer than a pin drop. Confronting the door, the twins open it and enter with caution. It's the opposite of what they expect to counter. No wild tiger attacks them in the entryway. Pure serenity. Peaceful, the opposite of their father. The whole main floor is sound asleep, and they assume their father is too while his bedroom door is closed.

On the same floor, the boys slink to their room with soft socks. When the door floats its back to the wall, the brothers halt. Dressers are knocked over. Mattresses are flipped upside down with their sheets all over the floor. The ceiling fan grinds its gears as its crookedness won't allow it to spin. The blinds had been pulled and ripped to the floor. Max's computer dissipates on the floor, littering it like a confetti explosion. The anger of their father loitered in the room, even in quietude.

Miles doesn't wait any longer. The heat inside the home doesn't flex right. He pulls out an unused suitcase from their busted closet and takes anything worth value to them anymore. Pictures of them with their mom and dad, more clothes, accessories, money from the safe, passports, school supplies, bathroom supplies, they even steal a little food from the pantry. Once they contain their necessities, Miles closes the door of the car for Max.

"What are you doing, Miles?" Max says.

"Stay right there," Miles says.

Miles reenters the home with a gift in his hand. He tiptoes into the kitchen. He digs through a drawer, taking a lighter with him. Behind the home is a filthy grill. He rests the gift on the open cooker, lights the grill up, and burns the gift as it melts in flame. He heads for the backdoor when his father bursts around the wall. His face is redder than the flame. Miles dashes around the house as his father rams through the backdoor. Max notices Miles marathoning it to the car.

"Get off my property, rodents!" the father yells.

Miles ignites the car and explodes with turbo from the house. As they speed along, Max's hair waves in the wind. When Miles' slides his window down, his hair sways too. They smile at each other, wooing down the street to their freedom. But Max realizes it may not be as it seems.

"We're running away from home," Max says.

"That place was never home," Miles says.

"But where are we going to live?"

"We both have student loans to worry about now," he says. "While we make a college team next year, after juniors here, we won't need to worry. As long as we're together, we'll feel at home. You're my home." There's a nice break for silence. They close the windows to allow the heaters to waft in hot air again. "Plus, we got friends who'll let us live with them."

"Liam?" Max asks.

"I don't think they got the space for us, but we're on a hockey team. I know a teammate on our team, a friend, who'll let us crash for a while. Does that sound okay?"

"I don't know," Max says.

"They got a bowling alley, an arcade, a movie theater, and an outdoor hockey rink on the lake," Miles says. "Why don't ya say we live a little?" Miles winks at him, reminding Max what he told him when they left the house in the first place.

"Okay," Max says. He hands the hotel card to him. "Deal."

The brothers lock their stresses of their father out from their lives. Sure, they don't realize how tough it is to live without a father, but maybe they're okay with it. They don't have a mother, which was hard for their survival beforehand. Every child should have the chance to be raised by their mom, but unfortunately, their mother didn't make it after they were born. She died from a c-section, saving her sons from missing the wonders on Earth. These twins shall thrive on.

Moms are heroes.

TOURNAMENT

Two days before New Year's Eve. Two days before I transform
my life into something more than I could have ever imagined.
These final hours I have are gonna be spent with my family and
friends. Barrett and I pay at the ticket stand for two adults. We're
handed our tickets, then we continue inside the front entrance of
Doug Woog's arena. The Knights play in the traditional Christmas
tourney inside. They won their first game, then lost the second
one. Their competing for third place tonight.

Before we depart the heat and into the cool, giant rink, food
engages our noses. In line for the concession stand, a chocolate
candy bar and nachos set on my taste buds. Barrett purchases our
food. He bought a candy bar with french vanilla cappuccino. You
can never go wrong with cappuccino. Kinda makes me jealous.

Through the doors is the giant arena. The bleachers stack on
top of one another as the floor ramps all the way down to the
bottom floor. A couple of kids roll water bottles under the

bleachers. They tumble to the hockey boards. Barrett and I continue forth, then walk across the top to sit near our parent section. Students usually don't watch the tourneys, but a bundle of friends still come and support, like Barrett and I, here to support Jake, Charlie, and Thomas.

Mom is on the bench, watching the Knights encircle Thomas and his net. They chant Knights after their pep talk. Jake and Charlie start out with their first line. The puck drops, and the action starts. I'm intrigued with the action for the most part, but these nachos and hot cheese smack in my mouth. I save the candy bar for last to trick my body into feeling full. Chocolate always has this mass to it when I eat it.

I wish Ash joined us, but he only has so much time before he's sent back to training camp. The day after New Year's, he flies back in the air to another world. At least the worst part of his training is mainly concluded. He'll be trained to shoot guns and learn skills for a special position he'll take place in when the time comes. But as of now, he visits with his family and other friends, healing his homesickness. I wonder if he received my letter I sent him. The military probably shredded it with their rules. But again, it is Christmas time, and they were sent back home.

Time soars through the rink as the game concludes. Jake scored a goal, and Charlie assisted. Thomas only allowed one goal in the intense game. They win the game three to one. The boys skate over for their third-place trophy and pile up like ants in the corner, pounding their weight on each other. Eventually, the crooks line up professionally for a nice picture. A snapshot memory I wish I had.

Kielstad Knights carry their victory into their locker room with mom. Barrett and I throw our trash away and huddle with smaller groups in the warm area, hinting at the popcorn that whirls out from the concessions. Popcorn never fails. Look at me, craving for food while I don't desire to work out quite yet. They ain't lying when they say the freshman twenty.

School is pretty simple for me and Barrett at the moment. Again, I'm lost on my paths. I'm ought to play college hockey, but I can't attend two colleges. Maybe I'll transfer instead but finding how to make a team worries me. And finding a team won't do much if I'm not an outstanding player, but I know I'm better than some of those other collegiate players. I just do.

The boys undressed, and mops of sweaty hair exit the rink. Jake and Charlie plow into us with their gear, saying their hellos to us. Mom appears around their bodies that sandwich us to the floor.

"Usually, you want to stay on your feet from a hit," she says.

Barrett giggles. Jake and Charlie leap off of us.

"Sorry, Coach," Charlie says.

"No worries," she says. "Ya had a good battle today."

Thomas joins our group. "Almost had a shutout, boys!"

"If only your defense was there to help," says I.

"Hey," Jake says. He nudges me on the shoulder. My smile wipes off as a joke to them. A pretty good one I have to say.

"Nah," says I. "That was a dirty goal. The kid was lucky to slip the puck between your legs."

"He lost the puck off of his stick," Barrett says. "The guy

tried to dangle dirty around you."

"It's okay," Thomas says. "These games won't go in the record book anyways."

"That's right," mom says. "This tourney was meant for fun and practice . . . And to keep you guys in shape from those Christmas cookies and candy canes."

"No one eats candy canes anymore," Jake says.

"They hurt my teeth," Barrett says.

"Frosted cakes are where there at," says I.

"You wanna ride with the boys back on the bus?" mom asks. "I can drive the car home."

"Barrett and I actually need to make a stop on the way back."

"Where to again?"

Barrett rolls the wheels up the driveway of the modern Victorian. We encounter the front door opening as we make our way up the steps to the porch. He welcomes us in.

"Clayton," says I. "It's so good to see you."

"You too, guys," Clayton says. An introductory hug invites us inside. "Take your shoes off, guys. C'mon in."

Clayton guides us to the living room where the ceiling spans up almost twenty-four feet. A balcony overlooks the sitting area. Huge glass pane windows face out into the darkness of woods.

"We saw your interview on the news the other day," Barrett says. "Well said."

"Thank you," Clayton says. "Better than my English presentation. I should show my teacher that for extra credit."

"You got one more year of high school to take in," says I.

"Enjoy it for as long as possible."

"For sure, man," Clayton says. "What are you guys up to?"

"I'm in pilot school," Barrett says.

"Oh, wow," Clayton's stepdad says, drinking sparkling water in a can. "You want to fly planes, eh?"

"Yes, sir," Barrett says. "Faced my fear of heights on a roller coaster." He smirks at me. "Now, I have to face my fear of calculus two."

"I'm always here to help you out with math," his dad says. "I'm a structural engineer. The math is fresh in my mind."

"That would be awesome," Barrett says. "Thank you."

"How bout you, Liam?" he asks. "Are you attending a college or have plans to?"

"I'm taking online courses right now, but I'm thriving to be a collegiate hockey player. So, I may transfer out. But I first have to find a way to get onto a team. I know I'm great at playing, just never got chosen from a scout."

"Well," the dad says. "Lucky enough for Clayton, he was handed two hockey opportunities. We took the college summer camp invite over the other one, but maybe I can get ya connected with the guy, Liam."

"Really?" says I. "Hands down, I'd aim for any opportunity for competitive hockey."

"Here's his business card." He hands it to me. "I'll let him know you'll be contacting him very soon."

"You don't know how much this means to me," says I. "Thank you so much."

"My pleasure."

"Congratulations with hockey, Clayton," Barrett says.

"Thanks, guys," Clayton says. "It was tough fighting for a spot while I had that coma, but I'm back on the grind."

"We're proud of your hard work," says I. "We wanted to visit you after everything to make sure you're holding up alright, and you should always know we're here for you."

"I appreciate that, guys," he says. "Thank you. Will I see you guys soon?"

"Sure thing," says I. "We should drive home before it's midnight, we haven't gotten much sleep, but we'll call you for some ODR or lunch or something."

"Awesome," he says. He stands from the couch as Barrett and I wiggle our feet into our shoes. "See ya guys, later."

"See ya," Barrett and I say. "Thanks, again."

"No problem, guys," the stepdad says.

He locks the door behind us as we start the car and leave. A nighttime drive soothes my mind. The city lights and soft rock on the radio makes for a nice drive home. While I relax back in my seat, I pull out the business card. Boe Lambor, manager of a hockey organization called Cryo.

Finally, my life presents a magical gift before the new year.

S'MORES

It's the Eve for new times. New goals and challenges bestow themselves for my tough achievements these past couple of years. I've met new friends, bonded with them through the pains and torture of hockey, yet we love it all and ask for more. The sport is more than a game, it's a lifestyle that keeps us sane and happy in life while we're family to one another. We fight battles every day to try and win the biggest wars. We sacrifice our body and bones to save our home. Nothing's more honorary than doing what feels good and enjoying the time with your teammates.

Barrett, Charlie, Jake, Thomas, and even Ash, are all at my house for the midnight celebration. Ash's parents and siblings came over to hang out with my mom and watch their son who's at home for the last day. He leaves tomorrow to complete his training for the Army.

Sparkling colors of juices fizz in their fake champagne bottles. We pour our flavored juices into our classical wine glasses, pretending to savor the celebrational alcohol. I believe the juice tastes better than the champagne does anyways. We've also filled ourselves with sugar cookies and pies, flavors consisting of chocolate extreme, key lime, and coconut cream. Shredded coconuts are like eating twine with whipped topping. But other than sugars, mom ordered pizzas earlier. Only one pizza remains. The slices will get eaten slowly over midnight here, unless someone's resolution is a calorie deficit.

"Boys," Jake says. "It's s'mores time."

"I don't think I can eat another bite," says I.

"No," Charlie says. "Not the food. Remember? It's what we called our pep talks in high school."

"Yeah," Jake says. "It's like a bonfire circle."

That explains a few things. It's funny how the past creeps up with me. No one ever told me anything. And as ironic as it is, our bonfire burns its glory in my backyard. Lucky enough, I was able to shovel the snow out of its pit, so the heat didn't melt the snow and wet the wood. The fire droughts the ground in its light. We settle on the surrounding lawn chairs, which sink their legs into the snow, and we prep for the talk.

"How does this work?" Barrett says.

"Well, we're gonna say our New Year's resolution," Jake says. "S'more talks are for us to be able to connect with each other's personal lives."

"Keeps us more like a team," Thomas says.

"Alright," Charlie says. "I'll start. Actually, both Jake and I have the same plan. We're gonna attend college up north in

Duluth, then we're hoping to play for an adult league for fun."

"That's great," says I. "You guys aren't trying out for a college team?"

"Nah," Jake says. "We don't really want to go to that level. We just want to play."

"Agreed," Ash says.

"I dream of playing college hockey though," Thomas says. "My resolution is to be pulled to a D3 team, goaltend for them."

On to Ash. "If I can survive the rest of bootcamp, I'll be happy to earn some money at a job, and travel around the world if I can."

That leaves both Barrett and me. While I'm a little anxious, Barrett speaks first. "I hope to fly my first plane this year, even if it's a duster."

"That would be legendary!" Thomas says.

"Heck," Ash says. "Join the air force. They'll just throw you in a plane your first day."

"I wouldn't survive bootcamp," Barrett says.

"You already did," says I. "Camp Kelmo." All the guys overexaggerate their laughs around the fire. No one else would find that to be as funny as we do.

"Alright," says I. "I suppose I shall go." Their faces bounce in yellows and reds as the fire crackles the wood. I feel the trees listening with their hollows, and the owls and wolves staring at me through the woods, waiting for my magical resolution. "I don't just dream of playing competitive hockey, but I will play competitive hockey. I'm ready to play college hockey."

Barrett pats me on the back.

"You'll make it, Liam," Thomas says. "Just push yourself in front of those coaches. Show em your strength."

"Thanks, Thomas," says I.

"How are the twins doing?" Charlie asks.

"They're doing well," says I. "Living on their own, well, with a friend of theirs actually. They're doing just fine."

"Guys!" my mother yells out the door. "The countdown is starting now."

We rush through the snow, kicking back dust to the one's in the back. Our feet trudge and trudge through the thickness of the powdered sugar till we reach the heat. We all gather with our drinks in the air as the ball drops on television. Counting down the numbers, I realize the past will be left behind. As every second ticks by, my anxiety escalates. I feel fresher than mint yet nervous for what the future holds, but I know this year will be different.

"Five." Thank you, dad, for teaching me how to skate. "Four." Farewell to my high school memories. "Three." Rest in peace, Chester, Orson, Shawn, and Finn. "Two." Tschüss to the pain that built me up to this very moment. "One." And hello to my transformation. "Happy New Years!"

COLLEGE HOCKEY

Moments ago, Ash and I crossed over the sky bridge together. And now, I'm watching him from afar, tagging his Army bag at the luggage desk. He meets me at the front of the room, lit by the winter sun, warming the front entrance for a nice farewell. He hugs me as my chin rests upon his green Army jacket. Our spirits lock us together as we continue to hug it out. It's until we slowly leave the hug when we say our final words to each other.

"When's our next hangout gonna be," says I. And as he doesn't answer right away, my eyes force the tears out.

"I'll be back in three weeks," Ash says. "We'll hang out before you know it. And I'll be back as a soldier."

"You're my hero," says I. "Ya break me from my comfort zone. You make me feel free." Ash slips out an envelope. And on the front is the camp's address, written in my puny handwriting. "You got it?"

"Yeah," he says. "The camp sent it to my house. I read it."

"And what do you think?" says I.

"Absolutely," Ash says. "We can be workout pals."

"Yes!" says I. "And how bout the trip?"

"Yes," Ash says. "When I come back from training, I'll make some money, and we can go wherever you want."

"Oh, I'm going to miss you," says I.

"I love ya, Liam," Ash says. We strangle each other in another hug.

"I love ya too, Ash," says I. He grabs me in a chokehold and grinds his knuckle into my head. He laughs as I push him off. As he smiles at me, I chase him to the escalators. As he hops onto them, I stop at the bottom, watching him inch away to security. We stare at each other till he's at the top. Ash waves goodbye.

While I cry my way over the skybridge, I pull out Lambor's business card. On the back, I scribbled down the address of the Cryo company. I emailed him the night I received the card, and he sent me the address to talk about the hockey opportunity in person. Now's the time to do it while I'm in the cities.

While traffic held me up for a bit on the freeway, I ride through the concrete trees to a building near the Excel Energy Center. Cryo's headquarters. I park my car on a parking ramp and cross the busy street to the front doors. A bellhop opens the door for me. I say my thanks and head inside. I speak to the woman at the front desk.

"I'm here to see Mr. Lambor," says I.

"You must be Liam," she says. "Follow me."

She takes me down the marble-floored halls, twisting me

through the halls to a small seating area, right outside of his office. As I sit on this leather chair, cars drive by outside the huge glass windows. The sun keeps me cozy as I wait for this man. I haven't seen him in person yet. I don't know much about this opportunity, but I'm hoping it can get me somewhere with hockey.

My foot jumps up and down to a silent song, an intense song that is. I chew on the skin of my fingertips while I have nothing better to occupy my time with. No newspapers crinkle nearby.

The office door opens. Mr. Lambor, a big man in a business suit, waves me in. "Greetings, Liam," he says. "Come on in."

"Nice to meet you, Mr. Lambor," says I. He closes the door behind me. I nestle into the mahogany-leather chair. He plops himself on his chair, pulling back his suit so it doesn't rip as he sits. Sheets of paper and a pen rest on his desk.

"I hear you want to play hockey for us," he says.

"I'd like to take any opportunity that'll help me get into college hockey," says I.

"Great to hear," he says. He stirs his morning tea with a small spoon and takes a sip. "I'm happy Clayton's father shared our contact with you. We're looking for more players to join Cryo."

"I'm embarrassed to ask," says I. "Can you tell me more about Cryo and its organization."

"Of course," he says. "Cryo is a fresh league on the market. We're a young company, seeking out players who don't want to pay for the hassles junior teams offer. Hockey players shouldn't have to pay a business to play for their teams. That's what we like to call a scam."

"Players should be recruited based off their skills and strengths," says I.

"Very well," he says. "So, signing up for our league doesn't cost you anything. We're here to help you stand out in front of college scouts and coaches."

"Do you guys pick many kids up?" says I.

"We accept everyone who wants to play. Brackets are set up for players, and they'll play all summer long. It's enough time for colleges to notice you guys. But only many will make it through the levels."

"Levels?" says I.

"Players will need to pass their tests in order to proceed, showing us you truly do have the dedication to play college hockey," he says.

"Okay," says I. "Would this camp host us to stay somewhere, or would I have to drive to the cities every day?"

"We host you right here," he says. "Above us are many royal hotel suites you and a roommate would stay in."

A roommate. That's amazing. I can meet a new buddy. Play hockey again. This is the dream. "How long is this league?"

"Lasts from June to late July," he says. "Not too short, and not too long."

"Okay, awesome," says I. "I think you answered all of my questions. How would I register?"

"I have a few sheets for you to sign," he says. "I'll need your basic information. Name, birthday, weight and height, home address, phone number, email. Scribble down any health confrontations we should know about, then you're all set. We'd contact you in April."

"Okay, sweet," says I. He slides the sheets in front of me. I grab the pen and start writing my information down.

The doors slam open behind me, causing the pen to jump out from my hand. A boy, about my age, falls to the floor. Two security guards grab hold under his arms and lift him up to his feet. "Don't do it!" he yells at me. His eyes burn in red fear. They stare into my soul. "Don't sign it! Get out while—" A guard muffles his mouth with a gloved hand.

"Take him out, will ya," Mr. Lambor says. "Sorry, Liam. I'm not sure what that kid's problem is. Maybe we should do this another time if he startled you."

"No, no," says I. Although I'm hesitant, where will I ever get the chance to play in front of college scouts? No junior team wants me. My last chance could be this very opportunity in front of me.

"If you're hesitant, there is no need to rush it," he says.

"I'm good," says I. "I'm not nervous. I'm ready to play again." And although I should beware that there's something fishy in this organization, I've been through horror before. And I understand why that kid crashed through. That's the first test. They're attempting to scare me away, but it ain't gonna work on me. I've seen scarier.

I sign my name on the final sheets, registering to play again.

MEDALS

It's taken weeks to get here. This is the final week of Ash's training before he flies back home to me. I can't believe how this year is exploding by already. I'm at the gym now, working out at eleven at night. No one's usually around this time of night, and I work the best when no one's watching. I don't want to embarrass myself in front of others while pushing myself above my limits. There comes a time and a place to do that in front of people.

Today, I work out on legs. I like to start off with back squats to fry the legs up right away and mix in bulgarians too. I hate to call it a warmup, but that's how I start my leg day. It's nice to get the tough challenges completed first, then finish with cool down workouts. I squat two reps with four sets, my weight's average around four-hundred pounds. My max out in high school was four-hundred and fifteen pounds. But while Ash isn't here to spot me, I have to stay on the safer side. Hurting myself is the last thing I want to do for hockey.

After squats, I head to the yoga room and use my jump rope. Jump roping is a great workout, and for hockey players, jump rope sprints is where it's at. I sprint for thirty seconds, jumping in my whipped orb as fast as my momentum can handle. When I rest, I take a swig of water with my thirty second break, then jump right back into it. I complete one-foot jumps, forward and sideways line jumps, and high knees in my jump rope routine.

To finish the leg day workout, I sprint on the treadmill in intervals of thirty seconds, and then after ten minutes of that, I hop on the bike for ten minutes, completing my rough interval workout. The hardest part about the bike is how much resistance it puts on my legs. It never really gets easier, but it strengthens my courage and self-confidence.

Leaving the gym in my shorts, allowing my legs to breathe in the cold, I think about how Barrett's day went. Today, he brought his notebook and backpack outside with him for class at his private flying school. Him and a few of the kids were confused while most of their time was spent in the classroom. But their professor took them on a fieldtrip to the nearby crop fields. A flat plain covered in snow sparkled on the ground. And behind a giant garage, connected to the plain, drove out an aerial machine.

Barrett's heart skipped its beats. The few kids were gonna go inside of an airplane, a small duster, just what Barrett dreamt about at the bonfire that night. They got to go inside and practice starting the plane up. The kids had to go through their pre-flight checks, just the basics of aviation safety. Barrett enjoyed sitting in the cockpit, fascinated by the stars of buttons that constellated the walls and roof.

Mom coached another game tonight. The boys played in Chanhassen. Jake, Charlie, and Thomas approach the ending of their season as the weeks flare by. Their season is decent, not good enough to reach the state tourney, but that all depends how they play in sections. Anything can happen.

After the incidents at The Barn, I wouldn't be surprised if Danny and Ben never hang out again. Ben has moved on with his college friends already, and I'm assuming he's questionable with Danny and his emotions. But not even a gun will turn Ben over. He's still in life for himself. And Danny doesn't find fun in me, but I got my fantastic friends. They're all I need in my life. Hopefully, Danny realizes he should attend a college to stay sane in his life. He can create new friendships at school. College is the time to put yourself in uncomfortable situations, meet new people, and reach your destined dreams.

Me on the other hand, I'm hoping hockey leads me down the right trail. As I pull up the driveway to my home in the snow bounded forest, I head inside to the dark basement. The darkness can't scare me anymore. The Barn has taught me a lot about myself. And it has brought me closer to home than ever. I pull my hockey gear out from the dark.

It's time to play hockey.

END OF BOOK THREE

THE PENALTY TRILOGY

"Thank you for reaching the end of my first trilogy as an author.
Shout out my series to hockey fanatics and readers to help the
series grow while there aren't a lot of hockey stories out there."

~ Ethan Marek ~

Made in the USA
Middletown, DE
21 October 2021

50303468R00130